Husky Hero

Neil watched the husky circle, stop again, and raise her head to bark before turning and whisking away.

Then, faintly, Neil heard something else. "Listen!" he said sharply.

"I can't hear . . ." said Emily through chattering teeth.

"Shh!" Neil waved at Emily to keep quiet.

They both strained to listen. From somewhere deep in the forest ahead of them came an answer to the husky's barking. A weak, high voice that might have been the bark of a puppy . . .

Titles in the Puppy Patrol® series

Puppy Patrol®
Husky Hero

Jenny Dale

Illustrated by

Mick Reid

A Working Partners Book

MACMILLAN CHILDREN'S BOOKS

Special thanks to Margi McAllister

First published 2001 by Macmillan Children's Books
a division of Macmillan Publishers Limited
25 Eccleston Place, London SW1W 9NF
Basingstoke and Oxford
www.macmillan.com

Associated companies throughout the world

Created by Working Partners Limited
London W6 0QT

ISBN 0 330 48416 8

1 3 5 7 9 8 6 4 2

A CIP catalogue record for this book is available from
the British Library.

Typeset in Bookman Old Style by SX Composing DTP, Rayleigh, Essex
Printed and bound in Great Britain by Mackays of Chatham plc, Kent

Chapter One

Neil Parker gazed through the window of the aeroplane, narrowing his eyes against the whiteness of the clouds. "We must be nearly there," he said. "I can see mountain tops!"

His younger sister, Emily, put down her magazine. She had been admiring a picture of a team of huskies, a blur of grey movement as they pulled a sled across a snowy landscape. She leaned across Neil to look out.

"Oh, I can't wait to land. It looks brilliant," Emily grinned.

"You can say that again," Neil agreed as they descended further and a snowy mountain range came into view. It all seemed a far cry from Compton, the small town in the north west of England where Neil and Emily lived, and from King Street Kennels – the boarding kennels and rescue centre run by his parents, Bob and Carole Parker. King Street Kennels had seemed a lifetime away all summer.

He and Emily had spent the last two weeks in New York and Hollywood. Now they were on their way to the last place in the world that Neil would have dreamed of visiting – Alaska!

Neil looked thoughtful. They were going to be joining their parents and five-year-old sister, Sarah, at White Mountain Lodge, a centre for retired huskies, run by their distant relatives, the Simpsons. They'd got in touch through the King Street Kennels website, which had helped the Parkers find long-lost relations and friends all over the world.

"Can you remember the Simpsons' names?" Emily's voice interrupted Neil's thoughts.

"Er, the parents are called Russell and Kim," Neil said, "and their daughter's called . . ."

"Fran. I remember that one," Emily finished, peering through the swirling clouds below. "Oh, look at that! I can see the lakes! And it's supposed to be sunny just now – at least, as sunny as it gets in Alaska. This is going to be fantastic."

Yes, thought Neil, *it is*. And it wasn't just the weather he was thinking about. The thought of a whole kennel full of huskies sounded pretty good to him.

After the air hostess had left them in the bustling airport lounge, Neil looked around for his father. Bob Parker, tall, broad-shouldered and bearded, should have been easy to spot in a crowd, but there was no sign of him. Neil felt a moment of anxiety before he spotted a familiar face. "Mum!"

It was a good thing Carole was so tall. Neil dashed forward with Emily beside him, delighted to see his mother here. She reminded him so much of their life back home. A middle-aged man, shorter than Carole, stood beside her. He had sandy hair and a moustache, and wore a check shirt and jeans.

"Mum, Hollywood was brilliant!" began Emily, bursting to tell her mother about the most recent part of their trip.

"Fantastic," Neil broke in. "Prince wasn't there, but Max was working with this amazing dog called Stripes. How's Jake? Where're Dad

and Sarah . . ."

"Calm down," interrupted Carole with a smile. "You haven't even said hello to Russell yet. We can hear everyone's news in the car."

"Hi!" The sandy-haired man had a deep, friendly voice, and he greeted Neil with a strong handshake. "Did you have a good flight?"

"Great!" said Neil, watching as Russell lifted their rucksacks from the luggage trolley. He and Emily had heaved their loaded bags from the carousel with difficulty, but Russell carried them both to the car park as easily as if they were empty.

4

"My car's parked over here," Russell said loudly. "I'll just put the bags in the trunk. I had one of the huskies in the car this morning, so it smells a touch doggy. Don't suppose you guys will mind."

"Mind!" protested Emily, laughing, as she opened the car door. Neil and Emily looked at each other with delight. The warm, animal atmosphere of the car was the most welcome smell in the world to them. It made Neil think of King Street and the green "Puppy Patrol" Range Rover. It reminded him again of his dog Jake.

"Was Jake OK when you left, Mum?" he asked.

"He was fine," said Carole. "I e-mailed Kate back at the kennels yesterday and all the King Street dogs are as fit as can be. I'm sure Jake will be overjoyed to see you when you get back. But, in the meantime, he's making the most of Kate's and Bev's attention." Kate and Bev were the kennel maids at King Street. Neil knew he could rely on them to look after all the dogs as well as he could himself.

While Emily chatted about the flight, Neil looked out of the car window. In the distance, steep mountains rose against the sky, grey and green against bright blue. The mountains were dusted with white snow at the tips.

"Do you guys like mountains?" called Russell over his shoulder.

"Yeah, especially those ones," said Neil.

"Good," laughed Russell, "because that's where we're headed."

"Great!" Neil grinned. He gazed out as the car snaked up the winding road. The mountain slopes reached up steeply on either side of them. "I wish I could take Jake for a run up here. He'd love it."

"He'd scare the wildlife if you did," said Emily. "Look! There's something moving! Oh, it's gone. I thought it might be a moose. Or a bear."

"You'll see all kinds round here," said Russell encouragingly. "Caribou, moose, lynx – ever seen a coyote? It's a real good place for foxes too."

"Most of all I want to see a moose," said Emily.

"What about you, Neil?" asked Carole.

"I just want to see the dogs, more than anything," said Neil. "Are they Siberian huskies, or Malamutes?"

Russell laughed. "We have Siberians at White Mountain Lodge. They're most popular round here for racing and tourist trips. It sounds like you've been doing your homework."

"He's turning into a husky freak," said Emily. "And he hasn't even met them yet."

The car wove its way on to smaller roads. There was hardly any other traffic, and few houses to be seen. Neil leaned forwards and spotted a smartly painted sign by the roadside – *White Mountain Lodge Kennels – Home for Retired Huskies* – with the Simpsons' names printed below. Then they drove through open gates into a smooth concrete yard with a neat modern bungalow on the left and, on the right, a long rectangular building. From the chorus of barking and yapping coming from the building, Neil guessed it was a kennel block.

"Gets noisy round here!" yelled Russell as he parked the car.

"It's great," replied Neil, raising his voice above the din. "It's like this at home."

"And there's Dad!" called Emily. She ran to greet her father as he appeared at the door, smiling in welcome.

"That's a good tan you two have picked up," Bob remarked as he reached down to hug Emily.

Neil looked round. "Where's Squirt?" he asked.

"If you mean your sister," said Carole, climbing out of the car behind him, "she's bound to be in the kennel block. She's practically moved in there."

As if on cue there was a pounding of booted feet as Sarah rushed across the yard, hurling herself at Neil and nearly knocking him over.

"You're worse than Jake!" Neil gasped.

"You've got to come and meet Attu!" begged Sarah excitedly. She was pulling hard at Neil's hand with both of hers.

"Who's Attu?" Neil looked puzzled.

"Just a moment, Sarah. Wait till everyone's been introduced." Carole raised an eyebrow at a short, plump woman who was following Sarah. "Neil, Emily, this is Kim."

"Good to meet you," said the woman. Neil noticed that she had roughened skin and a mass of wavy dark hair. She looked like someone used to fresh air and an outdoor life. "I'm sorry you won't meet Fran just yet," Kim went on. "One of her classmates has a thirteenth birthday party today. She'll be here later."

"But you still haven't met Attu!" cried Sarah, who was now tugging at Neil's arm as if she wanted to pull it right off.

Russell laughed. "She sure loves that little

pup!" he boomed.

"Russell," said Kim quietly, "you're shouting again." She turned to Neil and Emily. "I figure it's to do with being up in wide open spaces so much, and working with those noisy dogs. Russell hollers all the time, and doesn't know he's doing it. Don't let it bother you. Are you guys ready to eat?"

Now that she'd mentioned it, Neil realized that he was ravenous, but he wanted to meet the dogs too.

Kim seemed to know what he was thinking. "The dogs will still be there after dinner," she said. "Fran will be back by then, and she can show you round the kennels. Right now you can put your things in your rooms and wash for dinner."

"But they haven't met Attu!" insisted Sarah.

"Sounds like a sneeze," whispered Emily to Neil.

"OK, Sarah," agreed Kim. "You won't be happy till they've met him, I know. Go and get him."

Sarah ran to the kennel block. She was back in seconds carrying a bright blue frisbee. Running and yapping at her heels was a puppy that looked like a large, fluffy snowball.

"Oh, isn't he gorgeous!" exclaimed Emily. "He's like a cuddly pyjama case! Come here, Attu!" She dropped to her knees and held out her hands. The little white husky bounded up to her and gave her a sniff and a lick. Then he whisked away to Sarah again, looking hopefully at the frisbee and wagging his short, fluffy tail.

Neil crouched down and called the dog to him. The excited puppy scampered from one to another, clearly loving all the attention.

"He's six months old," said Kim. "He's such a character. He and Sarah just adore each other."

"She bought the frisbee with her holiday

money," added Carole. "She's been running around this yard with Attu and the frisbee ever since we got here. She'd sleep in the pen if she had the chance. Kim, don't let her wear him out. He's still young."

"Why do you call him Attu?" asked Emily.

"He's named after an Alaskan island," said Kim. "The dogs round here are mostly named after places in Alaska."

"Makes a change from Fudge the hamster," said Neil.

"I help feed all the huskies," said Sarah proudly. "And I walk them. I know all their names, and they know me. I can tell you all about them." But Attu was barking for the frisbee again.

"All right, all right, Attu," Kim smiled. "Just one more game and then we're going in to eat. In you go, Neil and Emily. I'll help Sarah take Attu back to his mom. You can spend all of tomorrow with the huskies."

Neil smiled. A whole day with the huskies – he liked the sound of that. This trip was just getting better and better by the minute.

Chapter Two

They were soon seated round a large wooden table, where Neil discovered that Kim and Russell's idea of a family meal was enough chicken casserole, rice and vegetables to feed a small army. He didn't usually refuse second helpings, but this time he knew he couldn't possibly eat any more.

"Am I giving everyone too much?" asked Kim, as Emily gave up trying to clean her plate. "Up here, with the cold climate and walking all those dogs, we have healthy appetites."

"I suppose the dogs will need walking tonight?" asked Neil hopefully.

"They sure will. You want to help? You'll be very welcome." Kim smiled at him.

"I can show you where we take them," said Sarah importantly. Suddenly there was a renewed volley of barking from the kennel block, followed by the sound of voices and a car door slamming.

"That'll be Fran," said Kim, and raised her voice. "Fran, we're in here! Neil and Emily have arrived!"

Within moments, Fran appeared in the doorway. She looked like a younger version of Kim, and was wearing dark blue jeans and a brightly patterned shirt.

"Hi, guys!" she greeted them. "Good trip? Have you met the dogs yet?"

"We thought they could wait till you came," Carole told her with a smile.

"That sounds good. Just let me get changed, OK?" Fran left the room and soon came back in faded dungarees with her hair pulled roughly into a pony tail. "Coming?"

The kennel block was very like the boarding block at King Street, with rows of pens on either side of a central aisle. Each pen had its own wire-meshed run, and at one end of the block was a separate room where food could be stored and prepared.

As Fran opened the door of the block there

was a scrabbling of paws as dogs bounded to the wire mesh. They jumped up with wagging tails and searching noses, studying the visitors with their bright, intelligent, blue eyes.

"What fantastic dogs!" said Neil. He walked from one pen to the next admiring the strong, friendly dogs. Their luxuriant, soft coats were grey or white or a mixture of both, and there was a look of wolf about their well-shaped faces and pointed ears.

"They're big and noisy, but they have the loveliest natures," said Fran affectionately. She led them to the feeding station, where charts showing each dog's diet were pinned to the wall. Sarah was already getting bowls out of a cupboard. Neil could see how keen she was to show that she knew her way around.

"That's very helpful, Sarah," said Fran, and turned to Neil and Emily. "Want to help make some dogs' dinners?"

The barking grew louder and more excited as they filled the dogs' bowls with food and placed them in the pens. Eventually there was no noise at all except the gulping and snuffling of the dogs as they ate. By the time Fran and Neil had cleared up, Sarah was jumping up and down to reach the leads hanging on the wall.

"That's right, Sarah, time for some walks," said Fran. "I hope you folks aren't tired, because the huskies have heaps of energy."

"Do they make good pets?" asked Emily.

Fran's mouth gave a little twist. "They're sociable but, the trouble is, they're not really suited to living indoors. They're better in kennels. Needing so much exercise can be a problem too. Huskies have great personalities, but they're outdoor types."

The barking rose again to deafening levels as she took the leads from the walls. "We'll take a few of them up to the top field and let them off the lead for a run," said Fran. "Mom and Dad will take the rest. Yes, Sarah, you can bring Attu and Kiska."

Fran put a couple of leads into Neil's hands and opened a pen, where two grey-and-white dogs with gloriously thick coats were waiting eagerly, standing on their hind legs with their paws against the wire. "Meet Denali and Klondyke," said Fran. "They're strong, but they're well-trained and they'll do as they're told."

Neil could feel the pent-up energy of the dogs as he fastened on their leads and followed them out of the pen. Sarah was waiting at the door with little Attu, who was yapping with excitement. Beside them stood a small, beautiful, cream-coloured bitch whom Sarah called Kiska. From the way Sarah talked to them, Neil realized that Kiska was Attu's mother. Fran stopped to make a fuss of Kiska, who pawed at her for attention.

In the top field, which was at least three times the size of the exercise field at King Street, Neil watched the dogs in awe. Freed from their leads, the huskies looked as if they could race and play for ever.

"If these are retired dogs, what were they like when they were working?" Neil asked.

"This lot will soon be tired," said Fran. "Working huskies pull sleds on very long journeys, so they need incredible stamina. They just keep on running."

"Isn't it cruel, using them to pull sleds?" asked Emily.

"Only if the owners don't look after them properly," said Fran. "We get some like that. See that one?" She pointed to a dog who, Neil noticed, was carrying one hind leg stiffly. "She had an injury that wasn't properly treated. And Klondyke? He was in a bad way when we got him. Underweight and scruffy. His owner didn't

16

much care what happened to him after he was too slow for racing. But most of our dogs have had a good working life."

Neil watched Kiska rolling over good-naturedly, joining in with her puppy's rough play. "How did those two come to be here?"

Fran smiled, as if she liked to be asked about Attu and Kiska. "We haven't had Kiska long," she said. "And Attu was only little when his mother arrived with us, so we kept them together. She's lovely."

Neil watched Fran walk over to the dogs and stand where Kiska could see her. As Fran bent over and patted her knees, Kiska jumped up, nudged Attu away, and trotted to Fran's outstretched arms.

"Good girl," said Fran, fussing her. She looked round to Neil and Emily. "There's no point in talking to Kiska but I can't help it. She's deaf."

Neil sat on the ground beside the friendly husky, who rolled over to have her tummy tickled. "I once trained a deaf dog with hand signals," he said. "A retired sheepdog."

"Yeah, Kiska knows hand signals," said Fran. "She hasn't always been deaf. She caught some kind of infection around the time Attu was

born, and it seems to have affected her hearing permanently. The thing is, if you're running a sled team, you can't stand in front of them giving signs. You don't stand in front of a sled team, ever."

Kiska pawed at Neil's hand. "You want more attention, do you?" said Neil, rubbing Kiska's thick fur. "You're certainly a lovely dog."

"If I've got a favourite, it's Kiska," smiled Fran. "She could do with having a proper home – look at her, she's so affectionate! But these dogs are hard to place because they need so much exercise and Kiska's never going to be used as a work dog now. I'll be sad to see her go, but I'd like to find her a good owner."

She smiled at Kiska, who licked her hand. Neil knew what it was like to care that much about a dog. He found himself hoping a good home would be found, for Fran's sake as well as Kiska's.

They stayed in the field for a little longer, throwing sticks and balls for the dogs, until Fran patted her knees at Kiska and whistled for the others, and they headed back to the kennel block.

"What do sled teams actually do?" asked Emily as they made their way down the track. "I mean, what are they used for?"

"These days it's racing and sightseeing mostly," said Fran. "Around here, it's mainly sightseeing. You can get to places on a sled that you can't reach any other way. And the dogs are intelligent, so they love a challenge. A good sled team is just great to work with."

It seemed to Neil that Fran was speaking from experience, but she wasn't much older than he was. "Have you ever driven a sled team?" he asked.

"Oh, yeah," she said. "My dad taught me."

Neil couldn't help feeling envious. He imagined himself driving a sled team, and wondered if he would have a chance to be a passenger in a sled. Back at the kennel block, as he put down water dishes in front of the thirsty dogs, Neil imagined these beautiful creatures racing forward with the sled flying behind them.

When all the dogs had been settled for the night, Fran, Neil and Emily went back to the house. Sarah had said a long and reluctant goodnight to Attu and was now curled up on Kim's lap, listening to a story.

Bob glanced at Carole. "Has anything been said about tomorrow?" he asked.

"Not yet," replied Carole. "I was waiting for Neil and Emily to come in from the kennels."

Sarah looked up. "Can I go somewhere to spend the rest of my holiday money?" she asked hopefully.

"There's time enough for that, sweetheart," said Carole. "I know you're dying to spend your money, but it'll keep."

Sarah opened her mouth to protest, but all she could manage was a yawn.

"All this fresh air and running about with the pup," said Kim with a smile, "it's worn you out. I think you're ready for bed, Sarah. We'll finish the story tomorrow."

"But Neil and Emily are staying up," argued Sarah.

"Not for much longer," said Carole. "Early start in the morning."

"Why?" asked Sarah.

Carole smiled secretively. "Come to bed and I'll tell you," she said, gently leading Sarah away.

When they were out of the room, Neil and Emily turned to their father. "What did Mum mean about an early start?" Neil asked.

Bob grinned. "Yes, you'll have to be out of bed early, and you'll need warm clothes. You're going right up into the mountains."

"Great!" said Emily.

Neil felt a surge of excitement so strong it almost took his breath away. "Into the mountains?" he said. "Are we going . . . I mean, how are we getting there?"

Bob's eyes crinkled as he smiled broadly at Neil. "On a dog sled, of course."

"*YES!*" Neil punched the air in delight.

"And you'll need pyjamas, toothbrushes, and the rest of your overnight stuff," went on Bob. "I suggest you pack a bag tonight."

"You mean, we're camping?" asked Neil eagerly.

"Russell's booked you all into a log cabin way up in the mountains," said Bob. "You'll stay there tomorrow night and come back the next day. No point in coming all this way to Alaska if you don't try a dog sled!"

Neil remembered something that had been puzzling him. "Don't you need snow for the sleds?" he asked. "Won't the runners get stuck on the ground?"

Russell grinned at him. "Don't worry, Neil, we've got two different types of sled," he explained. "You're quite right, snow sleds do have runners, but the road sleds we'll be using tomorrow have little wheels so we can go along tracks without snow."

Neil sank back in his chair, his mind filled with the thought that tomorrow he would actually get the chance to see the huskies at work, doing the job for which they had been bred.

Before he went to bed that night, Neil stuffed a change of clothes, and everything else he would need, into an overnight bag. Tomorrow couldn't come soon enough for him. He turned out the light, listening to the occasional bark from the kennel block and wishing he could reach out and stroke Jake's head as he did at home in King Street. He wanted to fall asleep quickly to make the day come sooner – but the thought of tomorrow's adventure kept him wide awake long into the night.

Travelling in a sled behind a team of racing huskies – what a day it was going to be!

Chapter Three

It seemed to Neil that he'd only just fallen asleep when a volley of barking outside woke him up. He sat up, yawned and rubbed his hands through his hair, making it even spikier than usual. He was still trying to work out exactly where he was, and why he could hear so much barking, when someone hurtled through the door and landed with a bounce on his bed.

"Hi, Sarah!" Neil gasped.

"We're going on a sled, we're going on a sled, we're going on a sled!" chanted Sarah, bouncing up and down on Neil's bed. Her eyes were shining with excitement. "We're going to be just like Santa Claus. Get up, Neil."

"I can't," Neil yawned. "You're jumping on me." He could hear Russell's booming voice coming from the kitchen.

"You guys ready for breakfast? There's coffee, juice, bacon, rolls, waffles – do you guys like waffles? We've got a long run ahead of us today. You need a good breakfast inside you."

Neil shooed Sarah away, jumped out of bed, and pulled some clothes on. He looked out of the window to see Kim crossing the yard to the kennel block.

"Is it time for the morning feeds?" Neil asked as he ran into the kitchen. With the kitchen window open, he could hear even more barking. "Shall I help?"

"Eat first," said Bob firmly. "There'll be plenty to help with when you're finished."

Emily was already there, turning bacon in a frying pan. "Where do the sled dogs come from?" she asked. "They can't be the dogs that live here, they're all retired."

"Russell has his own sleds," Bob told her. "And he has a friend not far away who does sled trips for visitors, and lets Russell borrow his dog teams. That's why it's even noisier than usual out there – two teams of sled dogs all ready to go."

"Two teams?" said Neil. He'd been desperate to set off since he'd woken up, but he hadn't thought of any details. "How many of us will there be to a sled?"

"There's you, Emily, Sarah, Fran and Russell," said Bob. "And all the stuff you're taking with you. That's two sled loads."

"What about you? Aren't you and Mum coming?" asked Neil.

"No, we'll help Kim here," said Bob. "You can have our share of being bruised, jolted, and overturned," he laughed.

"But if there are two sleds," said Emily, "who's going to drive the other one?"

"Fran's driving one of them," Bob told her. "Don't look so worried. She's very experienced. She's spent all her life in husky country. Kim said she learned to bark before she could talk, and they thought she'd never learn to walk on two legs because she went round on all fours like the dogs. A bit like Neil, really!"

Neil grinned and finished his breakfast quickly, before dashing outside. In the yard he saw the long, low shapes of the two dog sleds, where Russell and Kim were carefully laying out straps and harnesses. Neil looked closely and saw that the sleds were on wheels, just as

Russell had described.

Beyond them was a scene that reminded Neil of films he had seen about polar explorations. A whole pack of huskies was milling about in the yard – some grey, some creamy like Kiska, some black-and-tan – all looking around them with bright, alert faces as they sniffed the air.

Russell, bending over a sled, looked up and shouted to Neil. "I can guess what you're thinking, Neil. It's husky heaven! You wanna help?" He straightened up and walked over to Neil. "Maybe you want to meet some of the

team? We put the best dogs in the front – they're the fastest and the most experienced. This one," he went on, patting a dog that looked very wolf-like, with a pale brown coat, "this is Cordo. He can lead my team with Yukon. And we'll have Shoo – come here, Shoo!"

A honey-coloured dog trotted over to him, his ears pricked. Neil bent to pat him. "Is Shoo a place name?" he asked. The dog raised his head and Neil scratched him gently under the chin.

"It's short for Shumagin," said Russell. "He's everybody's friend, isn't that right, Shoo?" He rubbed the husky's head affectionately. "He and Valdez work well together, so they can lead Fran's team. The younger ones go further back. Eagle!"

A slightly smaller, grey-and-white dog with a very thick coat loped towards him. When Neil bent to fuss him, his hands sank into the soft fur.

Russell smiled. "This is Eagle. He's only eighteen months old, but he's keen and strong. He's learning fast, aren't you, Eagle?"

As Neil patted Eagle, a movement far away in the exercise field caught his eye. He looked up to see a small blue dot sail through the air.

"Sarah's up there with her frisbee," he said.

Russell looked up and chuckled. "Yeah, she wanted to have a bit of time with Attu before the trip. She can't bear the thought of two whole days without him. They've got the field to themselves. I daren't let our retired dogs out until we have this lot out of the way."

"Don't they like the sleds?" asked Emily, who had come out to join them and was struggling to fasten a harness.

"Don't like the sleds?" Russell laughed so loudly it hurt Neil's ears. "They love them! At least, the ones who've had a good life in a team do. They'd all be fighting over who goes in front."

"It's a pity they can't pull sleds any more, if they still enjoy it," said Emily.

"Well, I let the fittest ones do short trips," admitted Russell. "Just a quick spin now and again. But a trip like this – two days over rough ground – they'd have to be real fit and strong."

"Like you, Eagle," said Neil, stroking the young dog's soft head.

"You show us what you can do, young Eagle," said Russell. "Let me just check all those harnesses. Neil, will you fetch your little sister?"

Neil found Sarah and Carole already on their

way down from the field. Sarah gave Attu one last cuddle, pressing her cheek against his soft white coat as he wriggled and licked her.

"I wish Attu could come too," she said wistfully.

"I know, but he's only little," said Carole. "You can look forward to seeing him again tomorrow."

Bob appeared from the house, struggling under the weight of the overnight bags, Neil and Emily's cameras, and a large plastic box which was packed with food. Neil helped to load everything carefully on to the sleds.

"Who trusts me to drive?" called Fran as she hurried across the yard, zipping up her anorak.

"I do!" said Sarah, jumping up and down with excitement. So Emily and Sarah climbed into Fran's sled, while Russell and Neil led the way in the other one as they set off up the long, stony road which led into the mountains. The wheels of the sled rattled deafeningly, and the sled jolted and bumped over the rough ground, but Neil was too excited to feel uncomfortable.

He soon realized why Bob had told him to take warm clothes. The cold air felt sharp but exhilarating as he sat in the speeding, open sled. Looking around, Neil saw the keen, panting faces of Fran's dog team running behind them. And filling the skyline ahead of them, stretching as far as he could see, were the mountains. The spotless snow on their peaks dazzled Neil's eyes, and he was glad Fran had lent him a pair of tinted goggles.

The sleds ran on through the barren grey and green landscape that Russell said was called tundra, leaving behind the lower slopes which were bright with flowering bushes. In a valley far below, Neil could see a lake which reflected the brilliant, blue sky and two dark, flickering shapes.

Looking up, Neil spotted two huge birds circling in the sky above them. "Are they eagles?" he called to Russell, pointing upwards.

"Sure are," he said. "Bald eagles."

The sled slowed to a halt. Russell squinted up at the sky as Fran guided her team of dogs alongside her father's sled.

"So why did they go bald?" Sarah asked from her snug nest in Fran's sled. "And how can you tell from here?"

"The feathers on their heads are white, but the rest of their feathers are black," explained Fran. "This makes the eagles look bald, but they aren't really."

There was a gasp from Emily. "What's that?" she exclaimed. "Down there – look – in the trees!"

Emily pointed across the bare tundra to the forest that dropped away down the side of the mountain. Something was moving in the trees.

"Just wait," said Russell quietly.

As they watched, a hunched brown shape emerged from the trees. It walked slowly along the edge of the forest, turning its head from side to side.

"A *bear*!" whispered Neil in amazement. "A real bear!"

"You guys are so lucky," Fran told them. "Your first trip, and you see a bear."

"Is it dangerous?" asked Emily.

"Not as long as it's down there and we're up here," said Fran.

Neil heard the whirr and click of Emily's camera as the bear lumbered down the slope and disappeared again into the shelter of the trees. "Will we see any more bears?" he asked hopefully.

"Maybe," said Russell with a grin. "Keep your eyes open." He called to the dogs and urged them forwards again. Fran's sled followed close behind.

A little further on, they reached a rocky plateau, and Russell drew the sled to a halt. "This is a good place to stop and eat," he said. "And the dogs will be glad of a drink."

Neil remembered that bulky water carriers and bowls had been packed in the sleds. He scrambled out and began to fill the bowls with water. When the dogs had been watered, Russell produced generous packed lunches from the plastic box, and they sat munching rolls as they gazed across the steep-sided valley.

"It feels like this is the top of the world," said Neil, breathing deeply.

Sarah twisted round to reach her bottle of juice. "There's—" she began, then stopped abruptly because her mouth was full. She swallowed hard and said, "There's a Father Christmas reindeer!"

"What?" Neil jumped to his feet. "Where?"

Sarah pointed to the ridge behind them. "There," she said.

Neil heard Emily gasp. A moose stood calmly on the ridge, its head lowered under the weight of its massive antlers.

"Wow!" whispered Emily. "He's so huge. I didn't know they grew so big!"

"Don't frighten it," said Sarah.

"I don't think it would scare easily," Neil pointed out. "Happy now, Em?"

"It's what I really wanted to see," his sister breathed, carefully aiming her camera.

"Does that mean you can go home now?" asked Neil with a grin.

"No chance," replied Emily quickly as the shutter clicked. Neil unpacked his camera, but he didn't take a picture. He was rationing his shots carefully. He wanted enough film left to take pictures of the dogs at White Mountain Lodge. Sarah was too young to have her own camera, and she'd want a photo of Attu to keep, and Kiska, of course.

It was a long break, as Neil and Emily wanted to watch the moose, as well as take photographs and eat their lunch, but finally Russell announced that it was time to harness the dogs again. Neil brushed stray crumbs from his lap and stood up.

"There's an easy stretch after this," said Russell. "Wide and flat. Neil, do you want to have a try at driving?"

Neil couldn't believe his luck. "You mean, me – driving the sled? Yes, please!" he gasped.

"And you can try driving Fran's if you want, Emily," said Russell. Emily looked thrilled.

"Can I have a go too, please?" asked Sarah.

Russell smiled kindly. "You're too tiny just yet, honey," he said. "The dogs are too big and strong for you. But you can certainly have a go when you're older."

Sarah didn't argue with him, but slowly she turned and went back to the sled, with her head down.

Neil had thought that driving looked easy when he'd watched Russell. It looked a straightforward combination of steering the sled, calling to the dogs, and shouting, "Mush" now and again to encourage them. He climbed eagerly on to the step at the back of the sled. Russell stood just behind him and showed him how to gather up the reins.

With a tingle of excitement, Neil felt the sled begin to move beneath him but, to his alarm, it seemed to insist on veering to the left. And at least one of the dogs – usually Eagle – kept falling out of step with all the others. Neil braced himself against the jolting sled and couldn't help grinning. *This is really happening,* he thought. *I'm really driving this sled!*

From the sled behind came a shriek of alarm,

then laughter. Neil was watching his own team closely and didn't dare turn round to see what was happening.

"All right, Em?" he called.

"I am if Fran helps me," she replied, "but I can't keep a straight line."

Suddenly, Neil's sled hit a large stone and gave a jolt that nearly rocked him off his feet. Russell laughed loudly in Neil's ear and, leaning past him, he grabbed the reins.

"Not bad for a first time," Russell declared. "I'll take over for the next bit. The terrain gets rough after this. It's easy to overturn if you lose control, even just for a moment." He glanced up at the sky. "Let's get a move on. It'll be dark before we get to the cabin at this rate."

They halted the sleds while Russell took over from Neil and, behind them, Fran took over from Emily. Neil looked back to see how far he'd driven. It seemed to have taken a lot of concentration for a very short distance.

"Can't I drive just a tiny bit?" pleaded Sarah.

"Sorry, honey," said Russell. "Your mom would kill me if I let you try it. You do understand, don't you?"

Sarah nodded, but her face was pink with disappointment and Neil thought he could see tears in her eyes. But then Fran pointed out a dark brown hare racing across the snow and Sarah whisked round to watch it. "Did you see that hare?" she exclaimed. "I'm going to look for another one!"

"You might be lucky," Russell shouted over his shoulder to her. "There seems to be a lot of them this year. Let's get moving, we don't want to be caught out on the mountain if there's any freak weather."

"What kind of freak weather?" asked Neil.

"Any kind. Thunderstorms. Snow."

Fran heard him and laughed. "We never get fresh snowfalls in summer, Dad!" she called.

"Never say never," Russell warned. "None of us really knows what the weather might do."

"I hope it snows," said Emily.

"You don't, believe me," said Fran. "But I'm sure it won't."

As they drove on, Neil felt the air become colder and he marvelled at the way the huskies trotted on tirelessly. As they reached the snow line, where the winter snowfalls never thawed, the landscape looked more and more wintry, with snow lying thickly below the trees to either side of the track. Just as Neil was beginning to feel uncomfortably cold, they drew into a clearing where the path divided in two. Pointing to a narrow track was a wooden sign that read *Pine Peak Cabins*.

"Are there lots of cabins up here?" asked Neil, twisting round to look at Russell. He had imagined they would be staying in one small hut, alone on the mountain.

"It's a really neat set-up," said Russell. "It's ideal for long sled trips. You'll soon see."

"*BEAR*!" shouted Sarah, so suddenly that Neil jumped. The sleds stopped. Sarah was swivelling around and pointing into the trees. "I saw another bear, in the trees! Look!" she cried.

Something was moving, but Neil could tell it wasn't a bear.

"But it's walking on two legs, and it's much thinner than the bear we saw before," Emily pointed out.

"Then it's a thin bear on its hind legs," insisted Sarah.

"I think it's a man," said Neil.

"It sure is! It's Seth." Russell stood up and shouted. "Hi there, Seth!" Birds flapped in panic from the nearby branches, but the man hurried away without answering.

"That will have scared any bears away," giggled Fran. Russell shouted again, but the

man had disappeared into the trees.

"He did look like a bear," protested Sarah. "I'm going to call him Mr Bear."

"He's really called Seth," said Fran.

"She can call him Mr Bear if she likes," said Russell. "It's a good name for him. He's a bit grumpy, old Seth, and likes to be left alone, but there's no harm in him. He likes being up here. He's a good dog handler. One of the best. It's because he was so good that everything kinda fell apart for him," he went on mysteriously. "But we can't stay here in the cold. Come on. We're nearly there."

The sleds moved on along the stony track, with Sarah straining forward for another glimpse of "Mr Bear". Neil found himself wondering about the shadowy figure too. What did Russell mean when he said Seth had been "a good dog handler . . . until everything kinda fell apart for him"?

Then suddenly the cabins came into sight, and Neil forgot all about the stranger as he looked forward to settling himself and the dogs into their new home for the night.

Chapter Four

The sleds rattled into a semi-circle of small wooden cabins set in a wide clearing fringed with pine trees. The two largest cabins stood in the centre of the semi-circle. *Reception and Shop* was printed on a sign outside one, while the other had two doors, one marked *Laundry* and the other *Games Room.* Beyond that was the familiar structure of concrete and wire mesh that, to Neil's eyes, could only be a kennel block.

Russell called the dogs to a halt. "This place is purpose-built for folks going out on sled trips," he explained. "Sledding is really popular round here. I'll just check in and get the keys, then Fran can take Sarah to the cabin. It's been a long day."

"I'm not tired!" insisted Sarah brightly, trying to cover up a yawn.

The cold had seeped through Neil's clothes, and he was beginning to think his legs would be permanently frozen from sitting still. He climbed out stiffly and went to the front of the sled. Neil worked his way down the lines, fussing over each panting dog in turn, and had reached Eagle by the time Russell returned. Emily joined them and they began the long job of unharnessing the dogs and settling them into the kennel block.

Neil was sure he could go to any kennels, anywhere in the world, and know his way around. He and Russell carried the food into the preparation room at one end of the kennel block, and Emily began to fill the bowls for the dog teams. It was a rewarding job to watch the huskies gulping down the food until the empty dishes were gleaming.

At last, locking the kennel door behind them, Russell led Neil and Emily to a cabin where a welcoming light glowed from behind red-and-white curtains.

As they approached, Sarah's grinning face appeared at the window. She waved, ducked briefly out of sight, and reappeared at the front door, hopping with delight. "It's like a Wendy house!" she exclaimed.

"Sure is," agreed Russell, stamping his boots on the doormat. Neil found himself in a very plain room where everything seemed to be made of wood – the walls, the polished floorboards, the table in the centre of the room and the benches around it. But there were also lots of bright red-and-white cushions and a comfortable-looking sofa and, in a corner of the room, a stove. The cheerful crackling of burning logs came from inside it and Emily ran across to warm her hands. Near the stove there was a sink and a worktop.

Fran stirred something in a saucepan and placed it on the hotplate on top of the stove. "I hope you don't mind eating out of packets," she said. "It's the easiest way, on trips like this. This is supposed to be . . ." she picked up a discarded packet, "beef casserole."

"It smells good," said Russell.

Neil went through the living room and discovered two tiny bedrooms with bunk beds. Sarah and Emily had already put their bags in one, so it looked as if the other was for himself and Russell.

"Where will Fran sleep?" he asked.

"In the sled," Russell joked, and Neil grinned at Sarah's look of horror.

"On the sofa," explained Fran. "It's a fold-down bed."

"And we've even got a real bathroom," Emily pointed out, opening a door. The bathroom was so tiny that Neil reckoned there was hardly room to move between the loo, the handbasin and the shower, but it was spotlessly clean.

"I wish I could live here for ever!" said Sarah.

"Clean, simple and basic," said Russell. "It's all we need."

"It's like a house on a Christmas card," said Emily.

Neil knew what she meant. Everything looked too small and perfect to be real! He went outside to help Russell collect more logs for the stove, which was doing an excellent job of heating the cabin and keeping the casserole bubbling. When they sat down to eat their supper, with the light from the oil lamps flickering around them, Neil knew what Sarah meant about wanting to stay here for ever.

Far off in the mountains, something howled.

"Wolves," said Fran, as she spooned more food on to their plates. "Don't worry, they won't come near us," she added, seeing the look of alarm on their faces.

"I wasn't worried," said Sarah. She finished eating and leaned against Emily.

"Are you tired?" asked Emily.

"No," said Sarah firmly, "but I'd better go to bed before you. Then I won't disturb you when I climb into the top bunk."

"That's very kind of you, Sarah," said Emily.

Russell made hot chocolate, and by the time they had finished it Sarah was so sleepy she had to be carried to her bunk.

Neil was woken early in the morning by sunlight falling on his face through the small, high window. He showered, dressed and went outside. His first thought was to go to the kennel block and see the dogs but, as all the other cabins still had their curtains drawn and nobody else seemed to be about, he thought he'd better not. He wouldn't be popular if every husky in the block started barking.

Neil wandered round the campsite for a while. Then he walked a little way up a narrow, stony path, and looked down through the trees to the sparkling lake in the valley below. He just wished Chris, his best friend from Compton, could see this amazing scenery. They'd been camping lots of times in England – usually in hard, lumpy fields full of thistles and midges, never anywhere like this. Neil returned to find Fran and Emily tiptoeing round the cabin, buttering rolls for their packed lunch.

"Shh!" they both said as he came in.

"Sarah and Dad are still asleep," Fran explained. "I'll give them a bit longer, then I'll fix Dad some coffee. He might let us take the sled out by ourselves."

Russell was half awake when Neil and Fran crept in with coffee and asked him about the sled. He sat up, yawning and rubbing his eyes. "Sure," he said. "Now, Fran, make sure you double-check all the harnesses so they're good and tight. Take it easy, and don't go far. Be back in an hour, please."

"OK, Dad!" Fran said. Neil wondered if Russell would finish his coffee before falling asleep again. A glimpse into the girls' room showed them that Sarah, pink-cheeked, was still deeply asleep.

"She was up late last night," said Neil.

"Yeah, we'll let her sleep," said Fran. "You ready to go?"

A sudden burst of barking told Neil that he

needn't worry about being the first to wake the huskies. Neil, Emily and Fran slipped quietly out into the cool morning and were soon harnessing the enthusiastic dogs to the sled. Neil and Emily climbed in and made themselves comfortable while Fran stepped on to the back and gathered up the reins.

A little way up the mountain, Fran pulled the sled to a halt on an exposed stretch of ground. She pointed down to where a few pine trees dotted the mountainside at the very edge of the forest. "D'you see down there?" she said. "If you look past those tall trees on the right, there's a cabin."

"Is there?" Neil narrowed his eyes and saw a wooden hut so well concealed that it looked like part of the mountain.

"That's where Seth lives," Fran told them. Neil remembered the shadowy figure they had seen yesterday in the forest, whom Sarah had named Mr Bear.

"Does he only stay there in the summer?" asked Emily.

"No, he lives here all the year round, whatever the winters are like," said Fran. "He's a real wilderness man. He's like a – what's it called? A recluse. Doesn't have much to do with people if he can help it, but Dad says he's a genius with dogs."

Fran drove a little further, then stopped the sled and got out. "We'll let the dogs out of their harness here, and let them play awhile," she said. "They've got a lot of sledding to do today, so we don't want to wear them out."

Neil and Emily jumped out and released the dogs. Then, with Fran's guidance, they found a boulder to sit on which gave them a perfect view of the mountains around them. It stunned Neil to think that, only yesterday, he had craned his neck to look up at these heights.

"Caribou!" called Fran, and pointed. "A herd of them!"

Neil and Emily looked up to where Fran was pointing. The reindeer were making their way slowly along the top of the ridge, standing out clearly against the skyline.

"Oh, I left my camera in the cabin!" cried Emily in disappointment. The three of them sat in silence, watching the slow, dignified procession of the caribou.

Neil suddenly noticed that there seemed to be fewer dogs milling around them. He counted heads rapidly. "We're missing a dog," he said urgently, realizing that he couldn't spot a

familiar, honey-coloured shape. "Where's Shoo?"

Fran looked round. "Has he gone missing?" she asked, her eyebrows raised in surprise. "They don't usually wander off. And Shoo's old enough to know how to behave himself. I hope he's not hurt somewhere. Come on," she scrambled to her feet. "Let's go and find him. We'll all shout."

They called and whistled, but there was no response.

"Let's split up and look in different places,"

suggested Fran. "We'll meet here again in ten minutes."

Neil decided to go down towards Seth's cabin. If he didn't spot Shoo on the way down, he could see if Seth was around and ask him if he'd seen a stray husky. Seth might not want to talk to him, but it was a chance worth taking. Neil didn't like the idea of telling Russell they'd lost one of his dogs.

Neil didn't have to search for long. He scrambled quickly down the stony path to the cabin, calling, "Shoo! Shumagin!" He was rewarded by a familiar bark as the missing dog bounded towards him from behind Seth's cabin.

"Good boy," said Neil with relief, bending to greet the husky. "You had us worried! Let's get you back to Fran."

Suddenly a voice growled, "Is he yours?"

Neil looked up to see a shabbily dressed man striding towards him. He realized it was the same man they had glimpsed in the forest yesterday. Seen close up, Seth was small and wiry with a lined and weathered face and a bristly grey beard. He looked old, but he moved across the rocky terrain very quickly.

"Is this your dog?" Seth demanded again.

"No," began Neil, "but I—"

"He shouldn't be allowed to wander off like that," the old man went on, as if he hadn't heard. "Good thing I was here."

"We only stopped to watch the caribou," explained Neil. "I'd better take him back now, before the others get worried."

Seth leaned forward, listening. "Are you English?" he asked abruptly.

"Yes, I'm on holiday," replied Neil. Seth fell into step beside him as Neil walked back up the path with Shoo at his heels.

"And you never saw caribou before, I reckon?" asked Seth.

"I never saw anything like that until yesterday," agreed Neil. "We saw a moose, and a bear, and two bald eagles."

"Course you did! What d'you expect to see up here? Circus horses?" Seth's voice was still harsh, but Neil saw that his eyes were twinkling. They reached the sled at the edge of the forest. Fran and Emily were nowhere to be seen, but the rest of the dog team was tethered to the sled. They barked excitedly when they saw Neil approach with Shoo.

"This your sled?" asked Seth, ruffling the fur of one of the huskies.

"It's my friend's. I need to let her know I've got Shoo back," Neil explained.

There was a trace of a smile on Seth's face. "I used to have one called Shoo, short for Shumagin," he said. "Fine dog. But after he died, I didn't want to start again with another one. Never thought I could live without a dog around the place, but I seem to go on all right on my own. You like dogs?"

"I love them!" Neil jumped at the chance to talk about his favourite subject. "We run a boarding kennels at home. My own dog's called Jake, he's—" Neil stopped and waved as Emily ran out of the forest. "Hi, Em! I've found Shoo! Tell Fran!" he called.

Seth looked at them closely. "She your sister?" he asked Neil.

"Yeah. Her name's Emily," replied Neil.

But Seth seemed to feel he was being too friendly, because suddenly all his surliness returned. "Make sure you don't lose any more dogs," he said shortly. "I only live up here because it's quiet. I don't want to spend all day rounding up strays." With a final pat for Shoo he stumped back towards his cabin.

Fran burst into the clearing, sounding breathless. "Have you been making friends with

Seth?" she gasped.

"I wouldn't say friends, exactly," said Neil. "He was OK. He seemed to like Shoo."

"Let's get Shoo harnessed up and get back," said Fran. "Dad will be wondering where we are."

The harnesses were becoming much more familiar to Neil, and he soon had Shoo ready to go.

"Track's a bit rough here," said Fran as they set off down the path. "Slow down, Shoo! Good boy. Take it easy, now. What's that?"

Emily gasped as a hare darted from the undergrowth and dashed across the track. The sled lurched to the right as Fran tried to avoid it. With the huskies scrabbling madly on the stony track, the sled tipped over and Neil was thrown to the ground, hearing as he fell the unmistakable yelp of a dog in pain.

Chapter Five

Neil scrambled free from the upturned sled, which had slewed sideways on the rough ground, its wheels spinning in the air. Fran was already on her feet, struggling to release Eagle from his harness. The dog's efforts to free himself, together with her shaking hands, made it almost impossible.

"I'll hold him," called Neil as he helped Emily to clamber out of the sled. He knelt beside Eagle, stroking his thick fur until the dog stood still. Blood dripped from a long gash down Eagle's right hind leg. Emily ran to the front of the team and talked quietly to the rest of the dogs, who were whining anxiously and pulling at their harnesses.

"It looks bad," said Fran. The young husky had stopped whimpering, but he held the gashed leg awkwardly.

"I don't think it's deep," said Neil, examining the darkly stained fur. "The bleeding makes it look worse than it is."

"It's my fault," said Fran, and her voice was tense with worry. "I didn't react fast enough."

"Fran, it was just an accident," Emily said comfortingly. "You coped really well. You couldn't help the hare running out."

Fran nodded. "You never know what's going

to happen," she agreed. "But I should have kept better control of the sled. Are you guys OK?"

"I'm fine," said Neil.

"And me," said Emily.

Neil stroked Eagle's flank. "This is the only dog who got hurt," he said. "The rest of them seem OK."

"Eagle's young," said Fran. "He panicked when the sled went over. What will Dad say?"

She had turned very pale, and Emily put an arm round her. "We'll tell your dad it wasn't your fault," Emily said.

"Meanwhile, do you think we can get back to the cabin?" asked Neil. "Eagle can't pull the sled."

"I can manage with the rest of the dogs if I take it slowly," said Fran. "We could put Eagle in the sled to take him back, but the others would have to pull more weight with one less on the team."

"It might be a rough ride for Eagle too," said Emily, sounding concerned. "It could make his leg worse."

Neil had a sudden thought. "Seth's not far!" he said. "If Eagle can manage on three legs, I can take him down to Seth's cabin. I'll explain what happened, and ask Seth to look after him until your dad gets there."

"Shall I come too?" said Emily.

"Fran might need your help with the dogs," said Neil. "You'd better stay with the sled." He bent to pat Eagle's head and looked into the trusting blue eyes. "Come on, Eagle," he said. "We'll take it at your pace."

Neil walked away from the overturned sled very slowly, so that Eagle could keep up. The path down to the cabin sloped steeply in places, but Eagle hopped steadily beside him.

From the scowl on Seth's face when he opened the door, Neil could see he wasn't pleased to be disturbed for the second time that day.

"Sorry to bother you again," Neil began, "but I've got an injured dog here, and—"

"I can see he's injured!" barked Seth. "What you been doing with him?" He squatted down and examined the cut. Eagle stood still, submitting himself patiently to Seth's gentle hands. "How did this happen?"

Neil explained quickly about their accident. Seth grunted. "Sounds to me like your friend shouldn't be driving that sled," he said.

"Fran's very experienced," Neil told him. "She was just unlucky. Her dad's been driving sleds

58

for ages, and he taught her everything."

"Who's her dad?" asked Seth, his eyes still on Eagle's wound.

"Russell Simpson," Neil told him.

Seth looked up. "Is that so? Does he still take on retired huskies? Good guy, Russell Simpson. Know him from way back. Knew his father." Seth patted Eagle. "You leave this dog with me," he said, standing up stiffly. "If that cut stays clean it should heal just fine, but you don't want him putting his weight on it. You want to stay here, Eagle?"

The dog wagged his tail hopefully at the

sound of his name, and Seth's old face broke into a broad smile. A moment later, though, he was frowning again. "You tell Russell Simpson to come up and fetch this dog in a day or two. He needs twenty-four hours' rest, OK?" Neil nodded, feeling very relieved that Eagle was in such good hands.

As he walked back up the path, Neil turned to give a last wave to Seth but Seth wasn't looking at him. He was bending over the dog, talking to him and ruffling his coat. Seth's smile and the light in his eyes left Neil in no doubt at all. However grumpy he might seem, Seth was very glad to have a dog around the place again.

"Slow down," said Russell when they returned to the cabins and Fran began to gabble out her account of the accident. "Take a deep breath and start again." When Russell had heard everything, including Neil and Emily's comments, he pursed his lips and nodded. "Well, these things happen," he said. "One injured dog is one too many, but at least it was only one. You haven't done badly, Fran. And Eagle will be just fine with Seth. Couldn't be with anyone better. Don't feel too bad about it."

"Told you," whispered Emily to Fran.

"Still, it's too far to go home if we're one dog short of a team," Russell continued. "I'll borrow one from the kennels here. They're always able to help."

"Where's Sarah?" asked Neil, looking around the clearing at the other cabins.

"She's still in the shop," said Russell. "She's trying to spend her holiday money."

"I'd better keep an eye on her," said Emily, hurrying off.

Neil grinned. "Hire an extra sled while you're there," he joked. "You'll need it for Sarah's shopping." But, following Emily into the shop, he found Sarah gazing at the shelves, empty-handed. Neil couldn't understand why. The shelves were filled with cuddly toys, snowstorm models, posters of huskies, wildlife jigsaws – just the things Sarah liked.

"Can't you see anything you'd like, Squirt?" Neil asked.

"I like everything," Sarah replied. "I can't decide. I love the cuddly wolf cub. But there's a fluffy brown bear too, and they're both so sweet." She turned to face Neil, her eyes wide. "Why didn't you wake me up this morning? I wish I could have come with you," she complained.

"You were fast asleep," explained Emily. "We wanted to let you rest."

"And you wouldn't have enjoyed falling out of the sled," added Neil.

"Yes I would." Sarah's eyes grew even wider. "Did you fall out? What happened? Did the sled turn right over?"

Neil told her briefly what had happened, stopping every time Sarah interrupted, demanding to know if the dogs were all right, and whether the hare got away, and if the dogs had chased it.

When Neil finally described how he took Eagle to Seth, Sarah interrupted him again. "I wish I'd met Mr Bear. He's a bit like one of those things you get on mountains – you know, when it's snowing – one of those . . ." she frowned as she hunted for the word, "those snowman things. I know!" She brightened up in triumph. "A bunny-bubble snowman, a Yuppy."

"Oh, you mean a Yeti!" laughed Emily. "An abominable snowman. But those are supposed to be in the Himalayas, Sarah, not in Alaska."

"He could be a grumpy Yeti," said Neil quickly, seeing Sarah's look of disappointment. "He doesn't like meeting people."

"I wish I had met him, all the same," said

Sarah. "I'm sure he's a nice old Mr Bear, really."

"Have you decided what to buy yet?" Neil asked her, impatient to get back to the dogs.

Sarah shook her head and led the way out of the shop. "I couldn't buy just one of the toys and leave the rest," she said.

Russell was walking towards them with Fran at his side. "You ready to go yet?" he called. "I've got us another dog, to get us home. I can bring him back when I pick up Eagle."

They harnessed the team and loaded up the sleds. Neil watched everything keenly as they sped away, determined to capture every moment in his memory. He had never even dreamed that one day he would be jolting down a mountain behind a team of huskies. He wanted to remember it all for the rest of his life.

"You did well to get Seth to speak to you at all," remarked Russell. His loud voice carried clearly above the noise of the running sled. "He usually disappears fast if anyone comes near him."

"It was the dogs he wanted to meet, not me," pointed out Neil.

"Yeah, that's Seth," agreed Russell. "Great guy. My father always asked his advice if ever he had a problem with a dog. Seth used to have his own team, and he was famous for the way he managed those dogs. He's always been shy with other people, but great with dogs. Then some TV crew turned up to make a series of programmes about working huskies. They tried to make Seth into some kind of celebrity – you know, the wise old guy from the woods. Seth hated it. In the end he wanted nothing to do with them, or with anyone else. Retreated to his hut up here. Stopped running the team when he got older. Keeps to himself."

Neil felt a rush of sympathy for the old man, driven away from the huskies and the way of life he loved by an interfering TV crew. "He reminds me a bit of a tramp in Compton," he said. "Sarah calls him Father Christmas."

Neil told Russell about the time one Christmas when the house had been full of dogs because the heating in the kennel block had broken down, and how Nick Christmas had come to look after the dog they called Titan. They swapped dog stories all the way back to White Mountain Lodge. Fran, Emily and Sarah followed in the other sled. Neil could hear their occasional cries of "Ooh!" and "Look!" as one of them spotted a hare or an eagle.

The journey back seemed much shorter than

the previous day's trip. All too soon the sleds were rattling noisily through the gates of the Simpsons' home, bringing Bob and Carole running into the yard to meet them.

"It was brilliant, brilliant, I saw a moose!" called Emily, jumping from the sled. Sarah ran straight to the kennel block in search of Attu.

"The sled was great!" said Neil. He ran to the head of the team and patted the thick coats of the panting dogs. "Well done, you! Dad, it was unbelievable, we saw caribou and eagles . . ."

". . . and I got loads of pictures of the moose!" interrupted Emily.

". . . and we drove the sleds . . ." Neil put in.

". . . and you should have seen where we stayed the night!" continued Emily.

Bob held up his hands and laughed. "One at a time, please!" he begged. "It sounds like you had a great time!"

In the evening, when the dogs had been settled for the night, the two families sat round the kitchen table reading and discussing plans for the next day. Magazines and brochures were scattered in front of them. Neil was deep in an article about husky teams, vividly reliving the journey in the sled.

"Anchorage is a long way," he heard his mum saying.

"But it's a short flight," Kim pointed out. "You could ring up and book tonight. If you've come all this way, you might as well go there."

"What's Anchorage?" asked Sarah, without looking up. She was drawing pictures of Attu.

"It's a big city," said Carole. "We're thinking about going there tomorrow. Anybody want to come?"

Neil and Emily glanced at each other and shook their heads. Neil couldn't think why anyone would want to visit a city when they could stay here with the dogs.

"I want to stay here with Attu," said Sarah.

"Is that all right with you?" Carole asked Kim and Russell.

"No problem," said Russell. "But you might not make it. There's a forecast for bad weather over the end of the week. We could get snow."

"Never!" said Kim. "We don't get snow in summer!"

"The forecasters reckon we might," argued Russell. He turned to Bob and Carole. "But you won't get many chances to go to Anchorage, and we're used to coping with bad weather here."

"Sure," said Kim reassuringly. "This is

Alaska! A little bit of snow won't hurt you."

"We'll go for it," said Bob. "Kids, are you sure you don't want to come?"

"We've had our day out," said Emily. "Have a good time!"

"Yeah," said Neil. "Enjoy it!" Nothing could tear him away from another day with the huskies, and he was glad his parents had the chance of a day out by themselves. All the same, he remembered Russell's warnings from the day before. *None of us really knows what the weather might do.* Neil hoped everything would be all right – but he knew he'd be glad when his mum and dad got back.

Chapter Six

Neil woke up reluctantly. His eyes wanted to stay shut, but somebody was shaking him. At first he thought he was still in the cabin on the mountain, but slowly he remembered where he was.

Carole was gently shaking his shoulder. "Neil? Are you awake yet?"

"It can't be morning," Neil protested. He propped himself up on one elbow, squinting at the curtains with half-shut eyes.

"It's very early," said his mum softly. "You don't have to get up. I just want to tell you that Dad and I are going now."

"Have a nice time," mumbled Neil, and forced his eyes to stay open.

"Have a good day yourself," said Carole. "Help Russell and Kim with the dogs. And I want you and Emily to keep an eye on Sarah. We can't expect the Simpsons to cope with all the dogs and look after her at the same time."

"No problem, Mum," said Neil, and yawned. "Have a good time in Anchorage." And he sank back into sleep, until he was woken by the sound of Russell singing heartily in the shower.

In the kitchen, Neil found Kim making waffles. "They were right about the snow," she said. "I can smell it in the air, can you? And just look at those clouds!"

Neil looked out. The yellowish clouds above the mountains looked heavy and threatening.

"It's a real shame for you folks," Kim went on. "You should have sunshine when you're taking your summer vacation."

"This is fantastic," said Neil. "Up here, in the mountains with the huskies, snow seems just right. Anyway, we had loads of sun in New York and LA."

When he entered the kennel block the dogs barked excitedly, eager to go outside for their morning exercise. Restless and inquisitive, they raised their heads and sniffed the snow in the air. The first flakes began to fall as they raced around the exercise field, but the huskies took no notice. Neil knew their thick coats would keep them warm. Huskies were perfectly suited to snowy conditions.

When all the dogs had been exercised and fed and the pens cleaned out, Neil left the kennel block and walked through the soft, heavy snowflakes whirling around the yard.

Sarah appeared at the door of the house, frisbee in hand. He could hear Emily saying something behind her.

"But I don't need my jacket on!" argued Sarah. "I'm not cold!"

"Put it on anyway," said Emily. "Mum said. You don't want to catch cold and spoil your holiday." And soon Sarah, warmly wrapped, was running round the yard with Attu as he chased the frisbee and snapped at falling snowflakes.

"I can't believe this is a summer holiday," said Emily, coming out to join Neil in the yard. She turned up the collar of her jacket as the snow fell more quickly. "Thank goodness Mum and Dad brought plenty of extra clothes for us."

"Look at Attu," grinned Neil, as the fluffy white puppy ran after snowflakes and shook the settling snow from his coat. "I don't think

he's got much of a clue about snow," he commented. "He probably can't remember seeing it before, so it's like a new toy. If it settles, he'll be completely camouflaged."

Neil waved at Fran who was bringing Kiska from the kennel block on a lead. "Kiska loves snow," she called. "I'm taking her for a really long walk. Do you want to come with us?"

"Great!" said Neil.

"Of course," said Emily. "Sarah, are you coming?"

Sarah thought for a moment. "Can't I stay here and play with Attu?" she asked.

"I suppose so," said Neil. "Stay close to the house, though. I'll let Kim know what we're all doing."

Once they reached the exercise meadow, Fran let Kiska off the lead and they followed her to a steep uphill track. Kiska hurried ahead to pick up scent trails.

"She's a real mountain dog," said Fran. "She could go on all day like this, putting her nose into every root and every burrow. She isn't suited to living in kennels with lots of old dogs, however much I like having her. She needs a home where she can have lots of attention. I sure hope she goes to someone who understands her."

"Your dad wouldn't let her go to anyone who didn't," said Neil. Letting Kiska go wasn't going to be easy for Fran, and Neil wished he could help.

He stopped after a steep climb and turned, breathless, to see how far they'd come. Kiska was still hurrying ahead.

"Doesn't the house look small from here!" said Neil. "And there's Sarah and Attu." The three of them shouted and waved at the two small figures leaping around the yard, but they were much too far away to be heard.

"I hope Seth and Eagle are getting on all right," said Emily, sounding concerned. "If this snow carries on, it might be days before Russell can get up there to bring him back."

"I'm sure Seth won't mind," said Neil, remembering how pleased Seth had seemed to have Eagle as his guest.

"I can't imagine not having a dog around," said Emily.

"Even better, dozens of them," said Neil with a grin.

After they'd walked for about an hour, Fran stopped and said, "I reckon we should turn round, guys. The snow's getting heavier. We'd better get back before the track gets frozen over." She waved and beckoned until Kiska noticed and ran back to her. "Good girl," Fran said, fondling Kiska's silky ears. "I know you're deaf, but you still like lots of attention, don't you?"

Neil found it a lot harder to go down the hill than it had been walking up. The snow was settling fast, making the steep path slippery. Slowly, they picked their way down with their arms outstretched for balance, watching the ground for uneven ruts and loose stones.

As they entered the exercise field, Neil saw

that the yard below them was empty. "I can't see Sarah," he said.

"I expect she's round the other side of the house," said Emily. "It must be more sheltered there."

"It's snowing real heavy now," said Fran. "I reckon Mom must have called her in. Look out, Emily, this stretch is very muddy."

As she spoke, there was a squeak, a slither and a bump. Neil turned to see Emily picking herself up from the ground. "You all right, Em?" he asked, hurrying to help her up.

"Yuck!" Emily groaned as she twisted round to look over her shoulder at her muddied jeans. "I'm OK, but I'm wet all the way through. I'll have to change when we get back."

Getting back to the house took longer than Neil had expected. The snow was falling so densely that it was hard to see clearly. It was lying thickly on the ground by the time they reached the house, and they had to stamp the snow off their boots on the doorstep. As he opened the door, Neil could hear Kim talking to somebody on the phone.

"You'd better get changed right away while I put Kiska in her pen," Fran told Emily. "Put those wet things in the laundry basket."

"And I'll check on Sarah," said Neil. "I'll just make sure she's all right, and not wearing Attu out."

He ran to the other side of the house and opened the glass door which led to the garden. Neil couldn't see his sister or Attu anywhere, and the empty garden was steadily filling with snow. Cupping his hands to his mouth Neil called Sarah's name, but there was no response. He dashed back inside as Kim was putting the phone down.

"Did Sarah come in?" he asked.

"Didn't she come in with you?" Kim looked surprised. "I checked on her a while ago and she was outside playing with the pup, like she usually is."

She looked into the sitting room and Neil ran through the rest of the house, calling Sarah's name into each room, but without any response. However much he told himself that she must be safe, he felt more and more worried as she failed to appear.

Emily emerged from their bedroom, looking anxious. "Sarah was in the yard when we were at the top of the hill," she said, frowning.

"Yeah, but that was ages ago," Neil pointed out. "She could have gone anywhere in that time."

"And we didn't look down at the yard," said Emily. "We were too busy taking care of ourselves to keep an eye on Sarah."

Neil looked at Emily's pale face and guessed she was blaming herself. "I'm sure she's all right," he said, wishing he felt as confident as he sounded. "She'll be in the kennels, I should think, settling Attu down."

In the kennel block he found Fran drying Kiska's paws on a towel. "Is Sarah here?" Neil demanded quickly.

"Isn't she in the house?" Fran replied, a look of worry crossing her face. "She hasn't been here, and Attu still isn't in his pen."

Neil ran down to the far end of the block, where Attu and Kiska's names were chalked above the door to their pen. At the sight of the empty pen, with Attu's blanket lying in his basket, Neil felt his heart beat faster. They weren't here, they weren't in the house, the yard, or the garden. If Sarah had wandered away from White Mountain Lodge, she could be anywhere.

Neil heard Fran behind him, and turned to see the fear on her face. He made himself think clearly. "There are other places we could look, aren't there?" he said, trying to picture the other buildings around the kennel block. "The woodshed, the garage . . ."

"Sure. I'll get all the keys and we'll search everywhere," said Fran. "We'd better get going, fast."

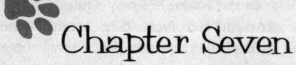

Chapter Seven

Neil and Fran ran quickly to the house to find the keys to the outbuildings. Kim filled Russell in about Sarah's disappearance, and a search began of every shed and outhouse and every corner of the garage.

From the centre of the yard, Russell put his hands to his mouth and roared out Sarah's name, his voice bellowing through the thickly falling snow.

Kim looked tense and anxious. "I should have watched her more," she said to Neil. "She was fine last time I looked."

"It's not your fault," said Neil, trying to re-assure her. "It doesn't take Sarah long to get into mischief. She never means to cause trouble."

"But she doesn't know her way around here," said Kim, and led Neil over to a corner of the yard near the garage, where there was some shelter from the snow. Her face was pale and she was twisting her wedding ring round and round on her finger. "Sarah could be lost, and getting more and more lost if she's trying to find her way back!"

"Couldn't Attu find his way home?" asked Neil.

"Depends where they are," said Russell, coming to join them. "If they've gone in some direction he hasn't been before, he could be completely confused. And he's young. We can't expect too much of him."

Neil remembered when Jake was a puppy. He had escaped on a snowy day shortly after he came to live at King Street. At the time, it had felt to Neil as if nothing could be worse than not knowing where Jake was, and whether he was hurt. But this was worse now. This time it was Sarah, lost in a strange place, in the middle of a freezing snowstorm.

"I'll go look for tracks," said Russell. He opened the garage door and reached for a coil of rope which was hanging from a peg just inside.

"I'll help," offered Neil instantly.

"Best if I go on my own, Neil," said Russell. "If there are any footprints at all, we don't want too many people tramping about obscuring them. You stay here with Emily and Fran."

Neil understood, but he wished he could be doing something useful to look for Sarah. He waited beside Kim, staring at the falling snow until Russell tramped back across the white yard, shaking his head. Fran and Emily ran over to join them.

"Snow's falling too thickly," shouted Russell, raising his voice above the wind. "Can't make out any prints. But you guys went up the hill, didn't you, from the exercise meadow? And you saw Sarah?"

"Yeah, she was playing in the yard last time we looked," said Fran, huddling beside her mum in the sheltered corner.

"And you didn't meet her on your way down," Russell went on. "So we know she didn't go that way."

"She might have fallen over in the snow," said Emily, who looked near to tears. "I did, and Sarah's only five, she's more likely to slip. She might be hurt or trapped or something, and it's freezing!"

"We'll take the snow sled right now and look

80

for her," decided Russell. "I've lived up here all my life and never seen weather like this in summer. Let's get the dogs ready. Neil, Emily, you come with me."

"I'll come too," offered Fran quickly.

"Sorry, honey," said Russell, "but that would be four to a loaded sled. Five, on the way back. Too much to ask of the dogs, and it would slow us down. Stay here with your mom, she's worried. We'll keep in touch by mobile phone. We may have to call out the emergency services."

Neil saw Emily bite her lip. "It might not come to that," he said quickly, putting his arm round his sister.

"OK, Neil," said Russell, leading the way back to the house. "Warmest clothes on. I'll get a team of our own dogs harnessed up. They don't do much sledding any more, but they'll get their chance today."

It was a miserable change from the excitement and anticipation of two days before, when they had first harnessed the dogs and looked forward to a day on the mountain. Neil patted each dog and whispered encouragement as he led them from the kennel block to the waiting sled. At the sight of the sled the dogs broke into loud, excited barking and beat their plumy tails against Neil's legs. Neil reminded himself that, retired or not, they were all experienced sled dogs. Their enthusiasm gave his spirits a lift, but the snow seemed to grow deeper every time he crossed the yard.

When the dogs were ready, Russell started checking all the harnesses. Neil was desperate to get out and begin the search, but Russell turned and went back into the house. Neil and Emily looked at each other in despair.

"Now what?" said Emily.

"Come and help carry some stuff to the sled," Russell called from the doorway. "Fran, do you have the kettle on?"

"The kettle?" whispered Emily as they hurried across the yard. "He's not going to stop and make coffee *now*, is he?"

"He must know what he's doing," said Neil, but he couldn't help feeling that every second took Sarah further away from them.

In the house they found Kim packing chocolate bars and biscuits into a plastic box. "If Sarah's trapped and you have to stay with her, you'll need emergency rations," she said, and her voice was tense with worry. "If anything happens to that little girl I'll never forgive myself. Your poor folks!"

"We'll find Sarah," promised Emily.

Fran was screwing the top on to a flask of hot soup. She looked up suddenly. "I know who can find them," she said, passing the flask to Neil. "Is Kiska in the team?"

"No," said Neil. "Should she be?"

"Take her with you," said Fran, and ran off to the kennel block before Neil could ask any more questions. Neil and Emily hurried after her.

In the yard they found Russell packing blankets and a First Aid box into the sled. "Go to your sister's room and find some of her clothes," said Russell when he saw them. "If she's wet through, she'll need to change."

"I'll do it," said Emily, turning back to the house. Neil hurried over to help Russell arrange the blankets in the sled.

As Emily ran from the house to the sled with some of Sarah's clothes in a carrier bag, Fran came out of the kennel block, shielding her eyes against the whirling snow. She had Kiska beside her on a lead, and she was carrying Attu's blanket in her other hand.

"Are we ready to go now?" asked Neil urgently.

"I reckon so," said Russell, looking down at

the supplies packed into the sled. "Get in, you two."

"And take Kiska," said Fran. "Let her run ahead. Her hearing might be gone, but she can still scent out her own baby." She knelt in the snow, one arm round Kiska, holding the pale blue blanket from Attu's basket. "It's no good telling her what to do," said Fran, her face close to Kiska's, "but she knows."

"She sure does," agreed Russell. Kiska was already sniffing the ground, pausing, trotting forward a few paces, and sniffing again.

"Hold tight," Russell warned Neil and Emily. He shouted to the dogs, and the sled began to move forward across the snow. They were heading towards the track they had taken two days ago. Neil was surprised by how smooth and silent the snow sled was, compared to the noisy road sled. The dogs' paws pounded against the snow, and the sled leaped forwards through the gate.

"Which way should we go?" called Neil.

"Main uphill path, until Kiska tells us otherwise," shouted Russell.

"Have you thought about why Sarah would just wander off?" said Emily quietly to Neil, as they sat snugly among the blankets and boxes of food.

"You know what she's like," said Neil. "Maybe she threw the frisbee for Attu and it went a long way, and she followed him when he went to get it. Then I suppose she just kept throwing it, and following Attu, until they were out of sight of the house. Sarah wouldn't think of the danger."

Emily didn't reply, and hunched herself up further against the cold air. Neil felt the sharp wind stinging his face. His cheeks were numb already.

"Hold tight," called Russell. "Kiska thinks it's

this way." He steered sharply to the right to follow the dog bounding ahead of them.

The sled swished along a path that Neil didn't recognize. He turned from one side to the other, looking out for Sarah's bright red jacket. "We'll find them," he promised Emily. "Look at Kiska."

Neil couldn't help feeling more hopeful as he watched Kiska bound along with her nose to the ground. The cream-coloured husky seemed almost as worried as they were. Suddenly Kiska paused, sniffed hard at a spot on the ground and circled it, then barked loudly before running on again.

"It looks like she's picked up a scent," said Neil. "I just hope it's Attu's."

Russell shook the reins and called encouragingly to the dogs. Neil felt the sled pick up speed. "Kiska's leading us uphill," he said, trying to work out where they were in relation to White Mountain Lodge. "But it's not the way we came the other day. I hope the dogs can cope with it."

The snow was falling so thickly that Neil could barely see the path in front, and there were times when Kiska was just a flurry of shadowy movement among the snowflakes. Neil

86

clenched and unclenched his fingers and toes to keep them warm, but it made little difference in the biting wind. He pulled his sleeves down over his hands.

Now and again they all called out to Sarah, but though Neil shouted until his throat hurt, his voice was only a thin sound lost in the vastness of the white mountains. *Come on, Sarah*, Neil thought, noticing that Kiska was leading them uphill across the snow-covered tundra.

Behind him, Russell was almost silent. He spoke a few words of command to the dogs but said nothing to Neil and Emily, as if he had forgotten they were there. Neil couldn't see his face, but he guessed it would be grim and hard with worry. Neil wondered how much of this trail the sled could handle. If the route continued as steeply as this, it might not get through at all.

We have to find her, thought Neil, his hands curled into tight fists. *Sarah, where are you?*

The sled slowed down at last, and came to a smooth stop. Neil looked up sharply. "Have you seen something?" he called to Russell.

Russell was leaning forward over the sled. "Look at Kiska!" he shouted back.

On the open ground ahead of them, Kiska was running round and round in circles, her nose to the ground and her tail held high. She raised her head and barked sharply.

"She's found something!" cried Emily. Neil jumped from the sled and ran as hard as he could through the snow.

"*Stop!*" yelled Russell in a voice like gunfire. "Stop right there!"

Neil stopped dead, and turned to look at Russell. He thought he had never seen anyone's face look so stern. Something was very wrong.

"Don't take one more step," Russell ordered. "Not in that direction. Come back towards me." He climbed out of the sled, telling the dogs to wait, and walked cautiously through the snow towards Neil.

"Can't you see?" said Russell. "No, I guess you can't in all this snow." He advanced a step or two ahead of Neil and pointed into the swirling snowflakes. "Now can you see?"

Neil leaned forward and did see. Kiska had led them to the edge of a cliff. When Neil realized how close he had come to falling over the edge, his legs felt like jelly.

"We need to check while we're here," said

Russell. "Get down and creep forward. Stop if I tell you."

Neil was glad of the chance to kneel down, though the snow soaked through the knees of his thick trousers. His legs didn't want to stand up any more. He crawled to the cliff edge and looked down into the steep-sided hollow.

Neil felt a surge of relief as he gazed over the edge. There was nothing on the ground below but a few scrubby little bushes, each covered with a thick layer of snow. No Sarah. No Attu.

Neil heard a satisfied grunt from Russell. "OK, they're not here," he said. "Kiska had me worried. But she seems to think they've been here."

Neil looked down again. Through the falling snow, at the bottom of the cliff, he caught a glimpse of a dot of colour.

It was a familiar shade of blue, half buried in a snowdrift. Neil recognized it, and all hope drained out of him.

"Look down there," he said, pointing. "It's Sarah's frisbee."

Chapter Eight

"**S**arah! *SARAH!*" Neil sprawled full-length on the snowy cliff top, bawling out Sarah's name.

Emily had scrambled out of the sled and was lying beside him, calling frantically. Neil could hear that her voice was tight with worry.

"Sarah could have been down there for ages. She could be buried under the snow," Emily cried. "She might be unconscious in a snowdrift!"

"Sarah!" Neil yelled again. He got up on to his hands and knees, feeling cold for the first time. He turned to Russell. "Did we bring any ropes in the sled? I could climb down and look for her."

"That's far too dangerous," said Russell. "If she's down there, we need to bring in the experts. I'll try the emergency rescue service. They'll send out a helicopter." He took out the mobile phone and tapped in a number. He listened for a moment, his face grave, and then he looked at the phone. Neil saw the frown on his face. The phone was dead.

"Can't get a signal here," said Russell. He banged the phone against his hand and tried again, turning one way and another in an effort to get through. "We're out in the middle of nowhere in a freak blizzard. There's no signal at all."

"Emily, are you OK?" asked Neil, almost as worried for her as he was for Sarah.

Emily had given up shouting for Sarah. Instead, she was clasping her arms round herself for warmth, and watching Kiska attentively. "We were so busy shouting, we stopped looking at Kiska," she said, sounding much calmer. "She knows best. Watch what she's doing."

Kiska had run away from them to the edge of the dense forest on their right. She was running backwards and forwards, sniffing the ground and circling with intense concentration.

"I think Kiska's found something," said

Emily. "Whatever it is, she's not at all interested in this cliff."

"You're right," agreed Neil, watching the husky carefully. "If she thought her puppy was in the hollow she'd still be up here on the cliff, trying to find a way to reach him. She'd be distressed. And just because Sarah's frisbee is down there . . ."

". . . doesn't mean that Sarah and Attu are!" finished Emily. Her face lit up. "Why didn't we see that straight away? She may have just thrown it too far and lost it!"

"And they've gone into the forest to shelter," said Neil, feeling hopeful again.

Emily ran to the sled and dragged out the bag full of Sarah's clothes. "Hold that," she said, pushing it into Neil's hands. She picked up Attu's blanket from the sled and ran over to Kiska. She held it out to the husky, who sniffed curiously. "Have a good sniff, Kiska," Emily urged her. "Good girl. Keep trying to find your baby."

"She already knows what Attu smells like," said Neil.

"Yes, but this will encourage her, as she can't hear anything we say," Emily pointed out. "Neil, give me something of Sarah's."

"You'll only confuse her," said Neil doubt-fully. "That's giving her two different scents."

"She can handle it," said Emily confidently. She grabbed a sweater from the carrier bag and held it under Kiska's nose. "Come on, Kiska. Find Sarah for us," she said.

Russell gave up trying to use the mobile phone. As he put it away, he watched Kiska closely. The husky's ears twitched. She raised her head and barked sharply.

"Whatever you say, girl," said Russell. "Neil, Emily, get back in the sled and let's see where she takes us."

Kiska ran a little way towards the trees, stopped, looked back and barked again. She stood waiting for them, her ears pricked.

"She knows what she's doing," said Neil. "She's definitely on to something." He helped Emily into the sled and jumped in behind her.

"She's heading into the pine forest, I reckon," said Russell. "That's good news for Sarah. There's more shelter in there."

Kiska led them far from the cliff edge. At first, the pine trees on either side of them were thinly spaced, but the path became darker and more densely wooded as the husky led them further into the forest. The snow which had lain so

deeply on the open ground was thinner here. It balanced on the treetops and occasionally fell in soft clumps to the ground.

Neil leaned forward in the sled. "Any sign of footprints? Pawprints?" he asked.

"Hard to tell," said Russell from behind him. Under the cover of the trees the snow was too light for prints, and the few places where water had collected were so muddy that no print could have lasted for long. Neil tried to watch both sides of the track at once, just in case he caught sight of Sarah and Attu moving under the trees, but Kiska seemed determined to keep up a fast pace. She bounded forwards and splashed through a shallow stream that ran across their path.

"Hold on tight!" yelled Russell. "We'll get across that, no problem!"

The dogs followed Kiska, sweeping the sled through the stream. Muddy spray flew into the air. Neil and Emily ducked, and Neil could feel his sister shivering.

"At least we can't get much wetter," he said, bracing himself as the sled bounced over the uneven ground. Suddenly there was a violent jolt, and for a moment Neil thought they would overturn.

"You holding on tight?" bellowed Russell. "Looks like the track's getting steeper." He shouted to the dogs. "Slow up, now, good dogs, slow up!"

"What's he doing?" whispered Emily in Neil's ear. "If we go too slowly we'll lose sight of Kiska, and she can't hear us calling her!"

"Yes, but we're going downhill now," said Neil. "The sled could get out of control if we go too fast."

"Do you think the sled could run into the back of its own dog team?" asked Emily.

"Of course not," said Neil, trying to reassure her. "Russell wouldn't let that happen."

Emily gripped the side of the sled as it lurched and jolted. "Ouch!" she said as her head banged against Neil's.

"Sorry about that," called Russell. "There's more mud ahead, so look out. Don't worry, we won't go through it so fast this time."

"Go as fast as you like," Emily shouted in reply. "We don't care how wet and muddy we are, we just want Sarah back."

Neil could see that the handling of the sled was getting more difficult all the time. The track was narrower than it had been, and growing steeper and rougher. The snow was thinner on the ground, which meant the sled moved less easily. Sooner or later, Neil thought, the sled would stick, or get completely jammed against a stone or a tree root. It was turning into a bruising ride for the passengers.

There was a fierce jolt. The sled stopped abruptly and Russell jumped out.

"Have you seen something?" asked Emily hopefully.

"No, honey," Russell told her. "But we can't get the sled any further. It's too much to ask of the dogs."

Neil stood up to look at the path ahead. There was a stretch so steep it would be a climb, not a walk, to get down it. Kiska waited for them, barking and circling and running to and fro urgently.

"I don't like leaving the sled," went on Russell, "but we don't have a choice. We'll just have to leave it here for now. The dogs will be fine. We'll go ahead on foot."

He pulled the box of food and the first aid kit from the sled. Neil scrambled out of the sled and turned to help Emily, who was still clutching the bag of Sarah's dry clothes.

"OK, we keep following Kiska," said Russell. "She thinks we have to keep going downhill. I'll go first."

Neil clambered after him down the steep stretch of scree, feeling loose stones slipping away under his feet. Beside him Emily lost her footing for a moment, and Neil saw her slip and land with a bump.

"Ow," she muttered. "Not again!"

"Are you all right, Em?" asked Neil. He stretched out a hand to pull her up, but she shook her head and scrambled to her feet without help. Neil saw that Emily was holding her right wrist with her other hand, and her lips were pressed tightly together.

Neil struggled across the path towards his

sister. "Are you hurt?" he asked.

"I put my hand down to save myself," Emily told him. "I landed hard, and it hurts a bit. I'll be fine. Can you pick up the bag of Sarah's clothes? And give me a hand to get down the next bit."

"It should get easier after this," said Neil, glancing ahead. Together they slithered down the slope, stumbling after Russell and Kiska.

"Kiska's getting faster," said Emily. "I hope she waits for us."

"She's getting excited too," said Neil, as Kiska started barking. The dog stopped, barked again, and ran on. "I think we must be close to them."

Kiska seemed to have more energy than ever. Neil watched the husky circle, stop again, and raise her head to bark before turning and whisking away.

Then, faintly, Neil heard something else. "Listen!" he said sharply. "Russell, wait!"

"I can't hear . . ." said Emily through chattering teeth.

"Shh!" Neil waved at Emily to keep quiet.

They both strained to listen. From somewhere deep in the forest ahead of them came an answer to Kiska's barking. A weak, high voice that might have been the bark of a puppy.

"It could just be a wild animal or something," stammered Emily, shivering, but her eyes were bright with hope.

"It isn't," said Neil firmly. He had no doubts. "It's Attu. I know his bark."

"Yeah, that's the pup." Russell scrambled back up the slope to join them. "And he doesn't sound too far away."

"Even if he is nearby, Kiska can't hear him," said Emily. She sounded concerned.

"But we can," said Neil. "And Kiska doesn't need to. She's really homed in on his scent now."

"It's hard to tell exactly where the sound is coming from," said Emily, still clutching her wrist. "Listen, in case Attu barks again."

They stayed very still, listening, but Kiska was barking so loudly they couldn't hear anything else.

"I think it was over there," said Emily, pointing with her good hand.

"She's gone!" called Neil in surprise because, as Emily spoke, Kiska turned sharply into the dark forest and, without waiting for anyone, completely disappeared from view.

Chapter Nine

"**W**here did Kiska go?" cried Emily. "She moved so fast, I can't see her now!"

"She went this way!" called Russell, setting off after her. "There's a way through here. Some kind of a footpath through the trees."

Neil grabbed Emily's hand and hurried after Russell, straining to keep sight of Kiska's pale shape as she bounded confidently along the winding path. "It's still downhill, but it's not so steep," he muttered to Emily. He didn't mention that, with the trees growing so densely, it would be easy to lose sight of Kiska.

"Where's the dog gone this time?" Neil heard Russell say. He had stopped in a small clearing, and stood gazing around him.

"There. In the shadows," said Neil, catching sight of Kiska trotting purposefully away from them. He turned to Emily. "It's slippy here. Do you want a hand?"

"I'm not helpless," Emily protested, but she still used her right hand gingerly.

Neil suddenly realized that in turning to help Emily, he'd lost sight of Kiska altogether. He saw that Russell was staring into the trees with a frown on his face.

Emily looked up. "Oh, Kiska hasn't vanished again, has she?" she said. "Why has she stopped barking?"

This time, Kiska did not reappear. For a sickening moment, Neil felt completely lost. They were in isolated mountains far from White Mountain Lodge. Only the dense forest protected them from the blizzard. Worse, there was no sign of Kiska, and she was the only one who seemed to know where they were going. And Sarah could be anywhere.

"Kiska!" Neil called, before he remembered it was pointless to shout for her.

"Sarah!" shouted Emily. "Neil, shout for Sarah, she must be somewhere near. Sarah!"

"Quiet!" said Russell sharply. "I can hear the dog."

Neil listened. To his great relief he could hear Kiska's urgent barking through the trees. They all turned towards the sound.

"There!" said Neil. This time he could see the pale husky clearly. She was barking as she pawed at a dark shape that blended in with the surrounding trees.

Neil looked again. "It's a door!" he yelled. "Look, she's found a shed or something!" Slithering on the damp ground, he ran into the trees, with Russell and Emily close behind him.

Kiska was on her hind legs, pawing frantically at the door of a timber cabin, so small and well camouflaged that, without her help, Neil knew he would have walked past it. He could hear Attu's voice now, and the puppy's high-pitched bark greeted him as he wrenched the door open.

The cabin was dim, but Neil spotted a familiar figure among the shadows. In a corner of the cabin, Sarah had wrapped herself in a sleeping-bag. Attu had curled up beside her, keeping her warm. They were curled up so tightly together that only Sarah's head could be seen over the white, fluffy shape of the young husky. Attu was whimpering with excitement. He wagged his tail in delight as Neil and Kiska burst into the room, but he stayed close to Sarah.

Drowsily, Sarah raised her head. "Hello, Neil," she said, blinking sleepily and closing her eyes again.

"Sarah!" Neil took her by the shoulders and gave her a little shake to keep her awake. He put his hand against her cold face. "Don't go back to sleep, Sarah. You're all right now, we're here. The sled's here. We can take you home."

Neil moved aside to let Russell kneel beside Sarah and he patted Attu. The puppy licked his hand. "Well done, young Attu," said Neil warmly. "You're a great little dog. You've taken good care of her."

Russell, too, put a hand on Sarah's face and checked the pulse in her wrist. "She'll be all right," he said. He felt Sarah's hands, buried in Attu's warm, soft coat. "Her hands are warm," he told Neil and Emily. "She's drowsy because she's cold and exhausted, but she's in no danger. If she'd been here a bit longer, or if she hadn't had the dog . . ."

"But she did have you, didn't she?" said Emily to Attu, rubbing his thick white fur. "Sarah, thank goodness you're safe. We were so worried about you," she said, hugging her sister. "Are your clothes wet? I've got some dry ones here. Your feet look soaking."

Emily had to struggle to get past Kiska to pull off Sarah's wet trainers and socks. Now that the husky had found her lost pup, she set about licking and nuzzling him in delight, but Attu still would not leave Sarah's lap.

"We could do with a blanket," said Russell. "I'll go back to the sled for one. I wonder where Sarah found the sleeping-bag?" He took out a flask from the food box which he had brought with him. "Keep Sarah talking and get her to take a hot drink. Try to keep her awake."

With a bit of help from Emily, Sarah sipped from the cup of hot chocolate.

"That's it, Sarah," said Neil, encouragingly. "Try to take a bit more." He stroked the top of Attu's head. "You're a brilliant dog, Attu, you're a hero. It's a good thing you found this place."

"It sure is," agreed Russell. "Neil, have you had a look at this cabin? It's been well looked after."

The light was dim, but Neil, staring round the hut, could see what Russell meant.

The cabin had only one room, and it was so tiny that with the four of them and two dogs it was crowded. There was more to it than Neil had noticed at first, though. "It's got a stove," he said. "It's like the one in the mountain cabin."

"Any logs?" Russell opened a cupboard door. "Say, look at this! There are blankets in here. Matches. Candles. Kindling." He shook out a blanket. "Put that round Sarah," he told Emily.

Then Russell disappeared outside for a moment, and came back with an armful of logs. "There's a log pile outside, in a shelter behind the cabin," he said. He pushed logs and kindling into the stove and lit it. Presently, the welcome crackle of burning logs filled the tiny cabin, and Neil felt warmth creeping back into his frozen toes and fingers.

Emily stretched out her hands to the stove. "Sarah's got a bit more colour in her face now," she said.

"Yeah, she could have been in danger from the cold," said Russell. "It's a good thing she had Attu with her, to keep her warm. When she's woken up a bit more I'll damp down the stove. Then we'll get her home."

Russell put his hands on either side of Attu's head and looked into the young dog's intelligent brown eyes. "Reckon you kept her alive, pup. I never knew what a brave dog you were."

"And he's only six months old," said Neil, full of admiration for the husky. He searched in his pockets for dog treats to give to Attu and Kiska, and watched with a smile as they devoured them.

"Yeah, just a pup," said Russell. "What's he going to be like when he grows up?"

"This cabin must have been put here just for times like these," broke in Emily thoughtfully, as she looked around. "An emergency shelter."

"Yeah, I reckon the rangers must have built it," agreed Russell. "Or some wildlife enthusiasts."

"The bears," said Sarah with a yawn.

"What do you mean?" asked Neil, puzzled.

"The bears built it," repeated Sarah. "Like in the story." She stretched, wriggled, and rubbed her eyes. "I'm sorry I got lost. I didn't mean to."

"We know you didn't," said Neil, who was just glad that Sarah seemed none the worse for her adventure.

"It's all right," said Emily, and hugged her sister. "Nobody means to get lost."

"We were playing with the frisbee," explained Sarah. "It flew over the gate and into the wood and I threw it again. It was fun. We kept playing and I think we just got a bit further away all the time. Attu always wanted one more throw. Then I looked round and I didn't know where I was. I tried to get back to the house, but I didn't know which way to go. We got lost. And I lost my frisbee, and it was my new one. Attu loved it." She sounded close to tears.

"Never mind that now," said Neil kindly, and hugged her.

"It was a good frisbee," said Sarah in a small voice. "I loved frizzing it."

Russell laughed. "Honey, you can have all the frisbees you can frizz, now you're safe and sound." He looked out of the window. "It looks like the snow's stopping now. You ready to go yet?"

"I'll try," said Sarah, but she wobbled as she got to her feet. Emily caught her, and winced with pain.

"I forgot about your wrist, Em," said Neil, jumping up to help them. "Let's see."

"It's OK, don't make a fuss," said Emily.

"Let me have a look, all the same," said Russell firmly. "Can you move your fingers?"

Russell examined Emily's swollen wrist in the light at the cabin door. "I'll put a tight bandage on it," he said. "We could use some ice to bring down the swelling, but packed snow will do."

"No thanks," said Emily, rolling down her sleeve again. "I've already been soaked through twice today. I've had enough snow in my clothes to last me a lifetime!"

Russell carried Sarah back up the stony slope to where they had left the sled. Kiska bounded ahead of them with Attu at her heels, as full of energy as if he was still playing in the yard. Neil and Emily scrambled up together.

As they reached the sled, the waiting dogs began to bark noisily. Russell put Sarah in the sled and wrapped blankets snugly around her. Emily climbed in behind Sarah, nursing her wrist.

"We'll give the dogs a drink before we go," said Russell, and Neil began filling the water bowls from the plastic container. "Then we'll get home as fast as we can."

When the dogs had finished drinking, Neil jumped into the sled behind Emily, but Russell hesitated. "I reckon it would be best if you drive for this first stretch, Neil," he said.

"Me?" asked Neil in astonishment. All he could think of was getting Sarah home as quickly as possible, and he didn't think his inexpert driving would get them back fast enough. "You want me to drive?"

"Just for this stretch," said Russell. "It should be easy if you don't take it too fast. Just while I see if I can get a signal on the mobile."

"Sure," said Neil. He climbed out of the sled and stepped on to the back where Russell usually stood. He glanced at the hill ahead of them. "At least, I'll have a go."

"Wish I could," said Emily with regret. "But I don't have a chance with this wrist." Neil could tell it was hurting more than she wanted to admit.

Russell climbed into the sled behind Emily. Neil shouted to the dogs and felt the sled move forwards with a jolt. At least the dogs were a lot more experienced than he was, Neil decided. In the sled in front of him, he heard Sarah saying that she was being bumped, and Emily quietening her. Russell was trying again and again to use the mobile phone, listening intently for a dialling tone.

It seemed to Neil that the dogs knew they were on their way home. They ran on smoothly, pulling together as a willing, determined team, their stride long and steady as Kiska bounded ahead. Neil called encouragement to the huskies, though they hardly seemed to need it. He felt much more confident this time, holding the reins lightly and leaning into the movement of the sled as it glided over the snow.

The sky cleared, the trees grew thinner, and at last there was a voice amongst the crackling on Russell's phone. Neil was concentrating on his driving so he didn't hear all of the conversation, but he picked up snatches of it.

"Hi, Kim, honey, it's me," Russell was saying. "Don't worry, we've got Sarah. And the pup.

They're fine. We're on our way back."

Russell tucked the phone into his jacket. "Well done, son," he said to Neil. "Pull them in now, and I'll take over. Good driving. I'll get us home."

Neil had enjoyed his chance to control the sled, but it was a relief to hand over to Russell with his smooth, fast driving. All of them were so cold and wet, they couldn't get home soon enough.

Chapter Ten

"Just get yourselves into this house and take those wet clothes off! Come and get warm! Sarah, honey, come here!" Kim came hurrying across the snowy yard and heaved Sarah out of the sled.

"Can I put Attu back in his pen?" asked Sarah through chattering teeth.

"No, you most certainly may not! Neil!" Kim called to Neil, who was on his knees at the head of the team, praising the dogs. "Neil, let Russell see to those dogs, you get in the house! I just had your mom on the phone. At least I was able to tell her you were all on your way home."

Fran ran from the house. Kiska bounded over to her.

"Well done, you clever, brave girl!" Fran rubbed her hands through Kiska's thick, cream-coloured coat and pressed her face against the fur. "Aren't you a wonderful dog!"

"She's done a great job," said Neil, struggling with numb fingers to loosen the harnesses of the other dogs. "So did Attu."

"Just leave that to me, Neil, I'll see to the dogs," said Fran. "You go and get changed."

"Yes, I will in a minute," said Neil, reluctant to leave the huskies. "Well done, you beautiful dogs. I wish I could take you home."

"Neil," insisted Fran. "Didn't you hear me? Dad and I will put them away."

"Before you catch pneumonia!" added Kim. But Neil, who had been looking forward all the way home to a hot drink and dry clothes, found he just couldn't leave the dogs. It would be unfair to go indoors before they were settled in their pens. He walked back to the kennel block with them.

"Oh, Neil," sighed Fran.

"He can't help it," said Emily.

"That's right," said Neil, and grinned at them over his shoulder. "It's all those years at King Street Kennels!"

Neil came out of the kennel block at last to

find Kim threatening to pour his hot chocolate over his head if he didn't come in at once and drink it. "OK, I'm coming," he said with a smile.

Fran had offered to stay and finish settling the dogs, and Neil guessed she really just wanted to be with Kiska. He left his wet boots on the step, came into the warm kitchen, and cupped his hands round the steaming mug. He sipped at the hot chocolate gratefully. "Worth waiting for," he said.

Neil felt even better when he had peeled off his damp clothes and changed. By the time he returned to the kitchen an inviting smell filled the air. Neil found that Kim had moved on from hot chocolate to soup and bread. Emily and Sarah were already seated at the table, and Kim was talking on the phone. "Neil, it's your mom," she said, handing him the receiver. "You talk to her while I get you something to eat."

As he took the phone, Neil realized that he hadn't a clue what to say to Carole. How much did his mum know about what had happened? Would he have to tell her that Sarah had nearly been lost in a snowstorm?

"Neil, are you all right?" Carole's voice sounded sharp with anxiety. "I've been hearing all about Sarah, and the snow, and—"

"We're all fine, Mum," Neil told her. "Safe and sound." But the tone of her voice showed him how worried she was. "Look, Mum," he went on. "I'm really sorry about everything. Sarah was all right, she was playing near the house, and then I thought—"

"Oh, Neil, don't blame yourself," Carole broke in. "We all know what she's like. Honestly, we need a lead for Sarah, never mind the dogs! I rang to say that your dad and I can't get back tonight. They've cancelled the flight because of the snowstorm, but we'll be back as soon as we can in the morning. We'll be on the first flight going out . . ."

There was a crackle of static and Neil found it hard to hear anything. He strained to listen, but all he could hear was Sarah asking Emily for more bread.

"Neil, it's a very bad line, are you still there?" Carole's voice sounded clearer.

Neil put one hand over his ear to shut out the background voices. "Sorry, Mum, the line broke up and Emily and Sarah were talking. I didn't hear what you said."

"I said we should be back mid-morning at the latest," said Carole. "See you tomorrow."

*

Neil was still tucking into breakfast the next morning when Russell came back from the airport with Bob and Carole. At the sound of the car, Sarah jumped down from the table and ran to the door.

Neil thought Carole and Sarah would never stop hugging each other. It seemed that everyone was trying to apologize for not managing to keep Sarah in one place, but Bob and Carole were so glad to be back safely and find Sarah unharmed that they didn't listen to any of it. Neil knew that sooner or later Sarah would get a serious talk about playing where people could see her, but there seemed to be more important things to talk about just now. Bob asked why Emily's wrist was bandaged, and Emily assured her dad that it didn't hurt at all.

Russell appeared in the doorway, putting his coat on. "I reckon we should go back up to Pine Peak cabins," he said, his booming voice drowning everyone else out. "Take the chance, while the weather's settled. I'll take their dog back, and see how Eagle's getting along. He should be OK to come home by now. You kids coming, or have you had enough of sleds by now?"

Neil looked hopefully at his parents' faces.

"Don't worry, Mum," said Emily. "I'll stick to Sarah like glue, I promise."

"Can we take Kiska?" asked Fran.

"Why Kiska?" asked Kim.

"I guess – I just want to take her," she said, and Neil understood. Fran was making the most of whatever time she had left with her favourite dog.

"Kiska would enjoy that," he said.

"But," went on Kim, "even if Kiska's going, Attu had better stay here. He had a long day yesterday, so I think he should rest."

"I'll bring him back a present," said Sarah. "Can I play with him just for a minute, before we go?" She ran to the door and sat down on the step to put on her boots.

Neil was pulling on his jacket and looking for his camera when he heard laughter outside. He ran out to see what was going on. He found Bob and Russell doubled up with laughter and Emily grinning broadly as she nursed her wrist. Attu was racing round and round the yard with something long and white trailing from his mouth. Sarah tore after him in pursuit.

"It's my bandage!" said Emily. "I just took it off to show Dad my hand was all right, and Attu caught the end of it and ran off!"

"Attu! Wait for me!" ordered Sarah, but the puppy took no notice of her.

"Well, it makes a change from the frisbee," said Neil with a grin. Dog-handling might run in the Parker family, but it looked as if Sarah needed a bit more practice.

The journey up to Pine Peak cabins was smooth and swift in the snow sled. Without their overnight bags and food for the huskies, there was plenty of room for them all to pile into one sled. When the borrowed husky had been returned to the kennel block, Russell asked if anyone wanted to go with him to see Seth. Neil hoped not everyone would want to go. He didn't think Seth would like to find them all on the doorstep.

Luckily, Sarah's attention was straying towards the shop. "Can I go in there?" she asked.

"I'll go with you," said Emily, and added to Neil, "Don't worry, I won't take my eyes off her."

The wintry weather had made the path down to Seth's isolated cabin slippery, but Kiska seemed to enjoy leaping over the snowy ground. When Neil, Fran and Russell arrived, they found Seth outside, chopping wood. The Simpsons' husky, Eagle, was with him, chasing woodchips as they flew into the air. He began to bark excitedly as Russell approached.

"What's up with you?" Seth said to Eagle. The old man looked up at Neil and gave him a nod and a grunt, but no smile. He jerked his head towards Eagle. "You folks come for your dog?"

Neil bent to meet Eagle as the young husky raced towards them. There was no sign of lameness now. Neil ruffled the dog's grey-and-white coat and smiled at his keen, intelligent face. He examined Eagle's injured leg. The healing scar looked clean and healthy.

Kiska, meanwhile, was sniffing at Seth.

"Nice dog, this one," said Seth to Fran.

"She's a star, but she's deaf," explained Fran, and began telling him all about Kiska.

Russell gave Eagle a final pat, and straightened up. "Looks fine to me," he said.

Seth shrugged. "Reckon he'll do," he growled. "I can keep him a day or two longer, if you want."

"No, we have to take him back today," said Russell. From the frown on Seth's face, Neil thought that he wasn't too pleased to hear it.

"He's a grand dog," said Seth. "Been good company. I'll miss having him round the place." He looked down at Neil. "Seen any more caribou?"

"No," said Neil, "but I did get a chance to drive the sled . . ." and he began to tell Seth all about Sarah's disappearance, and the rescue.

When he reached the part about the cabin, Seth's face creased into a smile. "And I suppose this cabin had a stove in it, and blankets?" he said. "Matches, maybe, and kindling?" There was a twinkle in his eye as if the old man was enjoying a secret joke.

"Have you stayed there yourself?" asked Fran, but Neil knew, from Seth's face, that there was more to it than that.

"You built it, didn't you?" said Neil. "You built that cabin!"

"Built lots of 'em," said Seth. "Here and there, in the mountains, in case folks got stranded. Go round them now and again, check they've still got supplies in them. Stay in 'em myself, sometimes."

"It could have made the difference between life and death for my sister!" said Neil. "She'll want to come and thank you herself."

"It was good to find her somewhere warm and safe," agreed Russell.

"Just as well it was there, then," said Seth gruffly. "I spend a lot of time in those woods. Built the cabins where I thought they'd come in useful."

Neil bent his head over Eagle to hide a smile. Seth didn't dislike people as much as he pretended.

"We should be offering you a reward," said Russell. "After what—"

Seth's face darkened. "What would I want a reward for?" he growled. "No use to me. Go on, take your dogs and go. Take care of them dogs, you youngsters. You don't know how lucky you are to have them."

The old man shook Russell's outstretched hand, nodded curtly at Fran and Neil, and gave a final pat to Eagle. "Don't work him yet," he told them. Then he turned to Kiska and smoothed her head. "Look out for this one," he went on. "She may be deaf, but I reckon she's got more sense than most people I know."

Seth straightened up and stepped back, still looking at Kiska. Neil knew that look very well. It was the look he felt on his own face whenever a favourite dog at King Street had to go home. It was the way Fran looked whenever she talked about finding a home for Kiska.

"Russell?" Neil began cautiously. "Kiska can't stay with you for ever, can she?" He glanced at Fran, and saw that she understood.

Russell studied Kiska carefully. "She needs space," he admitted. "She'd be happy here."

"And," said Fran, "I'd know where she was. If Kiska has to go, I'd feel better about her being here, with Seth, than somewhere far away with strangers."

"What do you think, Seth?" asked Russell.

"Well . . ." began Seth. "You mean . . . keep this one . . .?" He knelt down and held out his hands to Kiska, who nuzzled them.

"She needs a good home, and I can't think of

a better one," said Russell.

Seth straightened up and looked directly at Russell. "I would be glad to look after this dog for you, Simpson," he said, offering his hand to shake.

Fran knelt down, hugged Kiska, and gave her a dog treat. "Bye, Kiska," she whispered. "Be a good girl."

"She'll be fine here," promised Seth.

Neil and Fran watched Seth walk back to the log pile with Kiska beside him. The husky seemed quite happy to stay with the gruff old man.

Russell put a hand on Fran's shoulder. "Well done, honey," he said. "You made a good decision there." He turned and led the way back up the steep path to the cabins.

As they reached the reception centre and the shop, Neil saw two figures hurrying towards them. Sarah was staggering under several parcels. Neil quickly told Emily about Seth's part in Sarah's rescue.

Sarah didn't seem at all surprised when she realized who had built her cabin. "Seth? You mean Mr Bear?" she said. "I told you the bears built it. I bought him a biscuit, look!" From one of her many parcels Sarah produced a large bear-shaped biscuit.

"You can take it when you go to thank him," said Emily.

"And I can take Kiska her biscuits too," Sarah went on. "I bought some for her and some for Attu. Won't he miss his mum?"

"He's a big boy now," said Fran. "And he's still got all his friends at White Mountain Lodge."

Sarah reached into a large carrier bag. There was a burst of kindly laughter from Russell as she held up her treasure. It was a white, fluffy, large-eyed, toy husky puppy.

"It's Attu!" exclaimed Neil.

"It's just like him," said Sarah, rubbing her face against the fur. "I can't take Attu home, but I've got this one now."

"He's the next best thing," said Neil. "And he won't run away with bandages."

"He's mine," said Sarah, hugging it. "It'll make me think of him. He's my best ever dog."

Neil smiled. There was only one "best dog" for him. Neil knew that he would remember his Alaskan adventures for the rest of his life, but the dog he wanted to see most of all was waiting for him back home at King Street Kennels. Neil was ready to go home to Jake.